MW00942714

DARK HOPE

STILL SURVIVING BOOK 4

BOYD CRAVEN III

Copyright © 2019 Boyd Craven III
Dark Hope, Still Surviving Book 3
By Boyd Craven

Many thanks to friends and family for keeping me writing!
All rights reserved.

To be notified of new releases, please sign up for my mailing list at:
http://eepurl.com/bghQb1

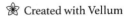 Created with Vellum

PROLOGUE

HOW WE LIVE our lives defines who we are. Every decision we make shapes and defines us as human beings. I knew every decision that led to every action of mine. I'd always acted in what I hoped was the right way, doing the right thing with my heart in the right place. Despite that, terrible things followed me. I'd shot Jessica and killed her father, then I almost killed her mother when she was out of her mind with grief and anger.

I'd analyzed every decision I'd made that got me where I was today, and I didn't know how I could have done any better. I wasn't normally a very religious guy, but somehow, I was starting to think the trials were personal tests. Not to see if I was worthy of heaven, but to define who I was, to me. What sort of man did I want to be moving forward in life? Since my grandfather was killed in the attack against the homestead and now Jessica had gone missing trying to meet up with her mother, I found myself alternating between anxiety and rage. Rage at KGR, or the Keggers, who'd made a pact with Henry, a man who betrayed his own people.

Together, they formed a coalition of dirt bags and degenerates that had started their own organizing and rebuilding process on the backs of slaves. The cops and former and current military members in the area were unable to put a dent in their numbers. I feared the worst. I'd heard screaming right before the radio went dead the last time I'd talked to Jessica, and I was afraid it was hers.

I'd tried to stay strong and spent a lot of time in introspection. How had a lowly moonshining family like mine become the focal point of epic level bad luck and insanity? Was my pathological urge and need to free others the Achilles heel of the group around me? I was starting to feel like a shit magnet. I was starting to think I needed to bow out of the equation to save everyone I loved.

Spider's KGR had made it plain they wanted me. Could I broker a peace by turning myself in? Would it save Grandma, my only remaining blood relative? Would they allow Emily and Mary the mercy they needed? I didn't want this for my life. I didn't want the trouble that followed me to spill over on everyone. If I left, I was certain I would still survive. How I would accomplish that, I had no idea.

WHEN I THOUGHT things were getting better, I was wrong. Again.

THE RADIO STARTED GOING NUTS AS EVERYONE WITH A radio at the farm got on the horn at once, asking about loved ones. I knew I wasn't going to talk over the chatter with this radio, so I took off at a dead run for the barn. People saw me coming and moved. I got in just as somebody was sitting in front of the radio. I grabbed the headphones and put them on, snatching the mic away from the startled woman.

"Sorry, she's calling me," I said, then keyed up the mic. "Silent Hunter here. Did you find the packages?"

"Yes," Jessica's voice said, sounding relieved. "More than we'd initially thought. Had to go radio silent for search and then bugout. Will you be ready for deliveries?"

"Yes, Yaeger's mom, copy that. ETA?"

"For me to know and you to find out." Her words were annoying, but I caught a tone of relief.

"Yaeger's mom, you're going to owe me."

The rest of the folks who had been clamoring to talk to Jessica had been trampled over with my transmissions, as the base unit had a lot more power and the big antenna to push signal farther. They had given up and gone silent as Jessica and I had been talking.

"I'll fix you some dinner, just as soon as... CONTACT—"

Gunfire came out of the speaker as somebody near her started screaming, then the transmission cut off.

I TRIED CALLING BACK REPEATEDLY. ALL DAY. GRANDMA and Emily stayed out of my way. I was going crazier, minute by minute. I raged at the world, I raged at God —I raged. I was careful to stay out of everybody's way; I didn't want to frighten the people who were all dealing with loss or fear of loss. I'd used the big radio, forcing my transmission over theirs as I had more power, a bigger antenna. They wanted updates on loved ones, as the base station in the barn had alerted them that things had gone wrong. They were waiting for details, as was I.

RAIDER AND GRANDMA WERE THE ONLY ONES WHO I LET get close to me. I knew my silent anger these last two days was hurting her, but I was absolutely consumed. I knew she'd lost Grandpa, her husband of about eleventy thousand billion years, but I'd lost him as well. I wasn't dealing with things in a rational way. I immediately wanted to go looking for Jessica, but they had been silent before that transmission and had been silent after that. There weren't enough people at the homestead to man every lookout point anymore, and not enough to man it all day long.

"You've got to eat more," Grandma said for the third time, pointing to my near empty plate.

I said nothing but took a drink of the coffee. I was thinking dark thoughts. They wanted me, they wanted Marshall. I'd never make the choice for the kid, but I was considering asking him if he would go with me if that was what I decided. It might stop the killing. Maybe they'd treat him the way they had before; keeping him in seclusion, but still feeding him. If he could avoid being hurt, would it be horrible of me to ask him to come with me?

"Please," Emily said from my side.

I turned to look and did a double take. Mary had crawled up on her lap, having awoke early. Both were red eyed, but Emily had wet streaks down her face.

"I'm not hungry," I said for the third or fourth time.

"You've got to eat something," Grandma said. "You've barely eaten since your grandpa's funeral."

Funeral. Was it a proper burial without a minister, pastor, or father? As a guy who hardly ever attended church, it was an odd thought for me. Sundays were the best day for making moonshine deliveries because most of the town and city was at church, and the busy bodies and gossips didn't have the ability to report my actions while they were saying their Hail Marys.

I dug into the eggs and fried rice that Emily had brought with fake gusto. I barely tasted it, merely shoveled it in, swallowed when needed. I felt hollow. Was fighting back the right thing to do? Of all the stories I'd read, movies I'd watched, I recognized the trope of the hero's journey that I thought we were all playing a part of here. We had objectives to overcome, bad guys to defeat, and a progression from the darkness to the light. Instead, the opposite was happening. Things were bad, and they were getting worse by the day. There were too many bad guys, and they were better than us in every way: better numbers, better equipment, better training.

When we thought we'd had a good defensive plan, we'd thought it had worked. It hadn't. They'd probably sent cannon fodder after us. When we'd tried to flip the tables, we'd walked into the same sort of trap that we'd used on them, but so much worse. It had at first been thought only two or three people had survived the raid, but Jessica's transmission had both given us hope, and then smashed our hope in the span of thirty seconds.

"Mister Wes?" Mary asked.

"Just call me Wes," I told her, forcing a small smile.

"Will you read me a story after breakfast?"

"I ... sure, what do you want me to read?"

"I'll go get the book," she said, sliding off her mom's lap and dashing to the bedroom.

Raider let out a woof and padded after her. He'd just about adopted the little one as his. It wasn't that he was betraying me, but he saw she needed something. Something more. When he wasn't at my side, he was at hers. Grandma told me it was his instincts; Shepherds were bred to herd their flock, their pack. He'd chosen her as part of his pack.

"I know you don't want to," Emily said, "but you've got to quit walking around scowling at everybody."

"What?" Her words startled me.

"You're walking around like you want ... it ... well, you're normally a very easy guy to like and get along with. Right now, though, you're scaring everybody."

"Why? Because my grandpa died? My girlfriend's gone missing, and half the homestead is either dead or the next thing closest to it!" My voice had risen until it was almost a shout.

Mary had been coming out of the bedroom with a book in her hand, but she ducked back in, slamming the door. Grandma reached across, her hand touching mine.

"Go ahead and yell at me! Does it make you feel better?" Emily matched my tone, my volume, her body tensing.

"Why does this have to be about me? I don't want to hurt anybody; I don't know what to do. And I grew up here. I'm sorry I'm scaring everybody. I just don't know—"

7

I'd stood up, but so had Emily. Instead of screaming in my face, she wrapped her arms around me, laying her head on my chest. She sobbed, and that, more than anything else, broke through my fog. I hugged her back, then ran my hand over the top of her head, smoothing her hair back. Then she let me go and slugged me in the shoulder.

"You big jerk," she raged, "it's not all about you! It's about *all of us*! For better or worse, you're kind of in charge around here, or at least that's what everybody thinks. You're falling apart, which makes everyone else think that we're all falling apart. Please, pull your head out of your ass long enough to see that we're all hurting here, but everyone is looking to you. They take their cues from you. If you give up, they're all lost, and they know it."

She punctuated that last bit by punching me again, this time not holding back. My arm stung where she'd gotten me, and my bad shoulder ached from the abuse. Grandma was sitting back, wiping her eyes and nodding along with Emily.

"But ... I don't want to be. I'm just—"

"Please don't hurt my mommy," Mary called from a crack in my bedroom doorway.

In her short life, she'd learned that yelling equated to pain. Pain usually reserved for her mother. I couldn't help it, I hadn't meant to lose control, but I was like one of the pressure valves on Grandma's canners. I'd blown steam off; I'd vented in a way I shouldn't, and now she thought her mother was going to be punished for it.

"I won't," I said, rubbing my arm and walking to her. "I'm just... I'm upset, sad, angry, confused." I stopped in front of my doorway, seeing part of her through the crack. "And I don't mean to yell at her or anybody. I'm just so..."

"You're sad, and you need to read me a book. That way we can both smile and feel better."

"You think so?" I asked her, seeing Raider push his nose in the crack, making sure an evil doppelganger hadn't replaced me.

"Yes, if you're done yelling."

"Come here," I said, feeling the tears welling up in my eyes.

I READ the story three times on the couch. Emily and Raider had sat at the table with Grandma, talking for a while. When Raider realized that he wasn't going to be getting any more scraps, he padded over and sat at my feet before laying down, letting out a big yawn.

"Thank you," Mary said, sliding off the couch. "Do you want to come to class with me today?"

"Class?" I asked her.

"Mister Marshall is teaching some of us to read more, and Miss Carla is working with us on math. She said she used to be a teacher, but she doesn't sound like one."

Carla ... was that the gal who'd lost her husband at the early attack against the homestead?

"I don't know," I told Mary. "Maybe some time, but I have stuff I have to get done today."

"Ok, take Raider with you today. He makes you happy."

She was right, and I would. Letting go of some of the anger and depression that had taken ahold of me gave me more room in my head to think of things. I needed intel, and I didn't have the usual people taking charge of things. I needed somebody constantly on the radio, monitoring things. I needed a census of who was here, who was missing, and what everyone's skillsets were. I couldn't do this all alone. Mary slid off the couch, leaving the book on the end table, then headed out, probably to start 'class'.

"You feeling better?" Grandma asked as I rejoined them at the table.

"Yeah, I... I'm feeling overwhelmed on top of every-thing," I admitted.

"You were acting like an unwiped ass," Grandma shot back, serious.

"I was," I said. "It probably won't be the last time it happens—"

Emily snorted. "What's that mean?"

"He's acting like a shit," Grandma told her, watching Emily burst into quiet giggles.

"We need to find out what happened and get reor-ganized," I told them. "I don't know who can do what for the most part. If we lost everyone in the party that went out,"—saying this made my chest tighten— "we're going to be hurting for manpower to do every-thing. I'm going to need both of your help."

Grandma raised an eyebrow as Emily's giggles tapered off.

"What do you have in mind?" she asked.

I told them, and they nodded in agreement.

"What do you have planned today?" Grandma asked.

"If I can find a big enough inverter, I want to get the well pump running in the house and get the solar panels installed."

"That guy who fixed the radio did that already; well, not the wires to the house. You should see if he'll finish things up, so you can concentrate on bigger things," Grandma said quietly.

"What bigger things? I... I'm not the leader you guys think I am."

"Yes, you are," Emily said, "and at heart, you're a good man. These things that are bugging you ... they wouldn't if you weren't. You know the difference between you and a monster?"

"No?" I said softly, scared to hear the answer. I'd felt like I was becoming one on more than one occasion.

"Monsters don't care about anything but themselves. We all have a bit of selfishness in us, but you're one of the most unselfish men I've ever met." Emily's words quieted me.

I wiped some grit out of my eye that the unmoving air must have blown in them and nodded. I got up and went outside, Raider following me. Lester was sitting in Grandma's rocker, polishing something small and metallic.

"Westley, how you doing?"

"I've had better days," I admitted.

"You look like you've got something on your mind. Need to talk?"

I sat next to him in Grandpa's spot. That realization hurt a bit, but I fought down the despair.

"I'm thinking I wish I knew more about reloading. Grandpa always did it. I want to find every suppressed gun in and around here and make sure I have enough ammo."

"You're thinking about doing some quiet work? Head hunting?"

"Something like that," I admitted.

"If an entire group can't go after the hostages and slaves, what makes you think you can?"

"The thought occurred to me that both sides are going about this in a conventional way. Guns, troops, entrenched defenses, armored vehicles..."

"And you're thinking unconventional?" Lester asked.

"Very much so. One or two sappers, snipers. Create havoc, move on to the next target. No major attacks, but make it hard for them to sleep, to eat. Make them wonder where the next bullet is going to come from. Who is going to come back from guard duty? Hit them at night, hit them in the middle of the day. Just hit them relentlessly and..."

"You know, Wes, I may not look like it, but I was in Korea during the war."

I stopped my ramblings and looked at him. He sat back, looking thoughtful. "So, you already know some of those sorts of tricks and traps used in defenses. They can be used in offensive as well. Set up your sniper's hide, take a shot or two, and when the assholes rush you in force, you're already gone but leave behind a surprise. Make them scared to even move, even after fired on," he explained.

"I ... tell me more."

He did, and although he was mostly describing tactics used against Americans by the Chinese who'd taken over the war for North Korea, I took notes. It wasn't the same as Vietnam, but a lot of the small-scale guerrilla tactics sounded familiar from reading history. It also turned out he was as much of a reloader as Grandpa was, something I'd forgotten. He asked what calibers I was wanting. I told him about the wildcat rounds my grandpa loved to shoot in the bolt gun and asked if he could be in charge of taking stock of what weapons and ammunition was left from the APC attack. He agreed immediately.

"You've got to see this, though," he said quietly.

The APC had been moved in front of the garage, and the trucks had had to play musical chairs. The explosion had killed everyone inside and damaged the interior. The guy who'd done the radio repair was going over it as much as he could, but with no schematics, nobody knew for sure. The ammunition for the big gun had all cooked off, but it was otherwise unharmed. I'd heard that much of what was inside, including the fire team, drivers, and gunner, had been all but turned into mush by the explosion. They were working to see what was salvageable.

"You've still got the 1911 you took from Henry's group?" Lester asked.

"Yeah?" I asked, following him into the barn.

Bits of equipment and clothing had been salvaged. Not everything had been destroyed, but most of it was trash. He walked over to a damaged pistol that had been put in the first stall of what had been the powder room. It was now empty; the dynamite had been used up in the attack. Weapons had been stored in here, and the kids were not allowed inside. There was always an adult watching.

Lester showed me a half-destroyed pistol. A suppressor had been sitting next to it. Like he'd practiced, Les took the top slide off the gun and then removed the barrel from the assembly. The threaded barrel was intact, and when he handed it to me, I saw it was clean. I held it up to the light, seeing that nothing marred the inside of the bore that I could tell with my naked eye. I grinned and pulled my pistol out, handing it to him handle first.

He worked his magic on my gun. After unloading it, he put the threaded barrel in and handed me the suppressor.

"Thank you," I said, making sure the gun was clear and working the slide a few times to see if it felt different.

"That's one quiet gun. I don't know if we have a holster for that. Now I know you love your grandpa's .22-250, but I can do the same thing with your M4."

"You've got a suppressor for one?" I asked him.

"The first fourteen who died attacking here? Yeah," he said, moving on down the line.

"The barrel is ruined," I told him, looking at it.

"Ahh, but the suppressor mount and suppressor aren't. They'll go right in that 1/2x28 threading your flash guard has. It'll hurt accuracy some, but I can see if I can Frankenstein a longer barrel if you're thinking of shooting at a distance."

"Les, how do you know all this stuff?" I asked him.

"From my time in the service, and most of it from afterwards." He held his hands up. "What? You think being a cutout for you moonshiners was the only scam I had going on?"

"You're ... a gun runner?" I asked him with a touch of hope.

"Former. Retired. Mostly to good old boys who didn't want the government telling them what they could and couldn't have. I did a little bit of machining back in my day, but most of it I had other guys do for me. I always played with things, but I wasn't a shooter. Not that way you and your grandpa were. If you're willing, I have a ton of 5.56 from what we've captured and what we already carry. I also have a ton of brass and my equipment ... and I can hand load some that I think are slow enough for the suppressor to work well. Or we could see if I could fit you up with a .300 Blackout."

"I... I'm a... What?"

"Tell you what, give me half a day and your M4. I'll round you up some subsonic ammunition one way or another."

"Mister Wes?" a little boy named ... Peter? asked from the doorway. "You going to go looking for my pa?"

"I'm ... yes, I am. I will be. I have to get prepared before I go. You doing class today?" I asked him, trying to change the subject.

"Yes, but we saw you come in here and well... I wanted to ask. My momma is working in the garden, and none of the other grownups were paying attention so..."

Note to self: make sure there's a grownup with Marshall. If Carla wasn't there, he's not a babysitter. He was practically a kid himself.

"You should get back to your studies," I told him.

"Ok. I'm praying you'll find everyone. We miss Miss Jessica too."

His words set off another pain in my chest, but I knew he meant well. I nodded and waved.

"So, you can do all of this?" I asked him.

"Yes," Les said, putting a hand on my shoulder, "but I don't want you going off half-cocked. People around here need you. I know why you want and need to do this alone, but right now, you're needed here. Your grandma needs you to come back safe."

"I know," I admitted. "I didn't want whatever job it is people want me to do, but I'll do my best."

"That's all we can ever do," Les said.

"How are folks holding up, food wise?" I asked.

Les leaned in close and whispered, "With reduced mouths to feed, it's not as bad as we'd thought, but we're always short on meat."

"You know where Grandpa had been using those rabbit boxes?" I asked Les.

"Sure," he replied. "Been resetting them every day. Sometimes we get lucky, sometimes not."

"Maybe that'd be a good thing for the kids to do in class. Little arts and crafts? Make some more?" I asked with a grin. "Learn to make a snare?"

"Hey now, you're starting to make sense. You been hitting the sauce again?"

"Not very much lately."

"Damn shame, I was hoping if you did, you'd share."

"I will, when I get back tonight."

"Where are you going?" he asked me.

"Back to the Crater of Diamonds. Mostly to gather my thoughts, but also to see if anybody's come back, and to maybe do a little hunting."

"Drop off your carbine before you go, or I'll put something else together for you entirely."

"Do we have enough guns to do that?" I asked him.

"Most of the folks who went out took their own equipment, and some folks here are carrying captured equipment, but there's not many of them left who are comfortable and knowledgeable about this stuff."

"Can you also help fix that?" I asked him. "I'm starting to understand that this is only the beginning of the nightmare."

"I'm not a shooter," Les said. "The finer skills like that are more you Flaggs' specialties, among other things."

I laughed. "I'm not a shooter. Just a moonshiner and a poacher."

"Who goes in silent, stalks game that has better senses than he does, and takes one shot to kill it immediately from close or far distances? Not everybody can do that. The military spends big bucks developing skills like you've got. I'm more of a ham and egger myself. I qualified for Uncle Sam whenever I had to, but I didn't have that special something."

"I'm not a great teacher," I told him, "and you know the weapon platforms far better than me. Let's take this one step at a time."

Les nodded, a smile breaking his stoic features.

3

I WASN'T SERIOUSLY HUNTING; I'd taken my dog with
me. I'd also taken my usual poaching gear, my pack
full of my camo netting, cordage, my canteen, my usual
supplies, and half a days' worth of food Grandma had
packed. I had Grandpa's suppressed bolt gun over my
shoulder and the modified 1911 on my hip. It had taken
some expert cutting and sewing on Grandma's part,
but the gun was holstered at my side now. I'd also
taken a radio which I'd left off, and the night vision I'd
lifted forever ago along with my binoculars.

I'd told Emily and Grandma my plans, and they'd
just nodded. No questions or arguments. Were they
right? Were Lester, Emily, and Grandma, right? Why
had I got this damned job? That thought went over and
over in my head as I walked. Raider was padding along
next to me on silent feet, falling back when the trail
narrowed. I wouldn't be on the trail long, though; trails
were where the possum sheriffs and ATF goons staged

their ambushes. I figured the Keggers would be of like mind.

After walking past our last unmanned lookout point, I got off trail and started walking softly, slowly. Heel to toe, watching every step, making sure I minimized sound, smelling the air for any indication or clues. By habit, I walked so my scent wouldn't be carried downwind to the area I was planning to stalk.

It was a good twenty minutes into the slow going that Raider went still, a low rumble coming out of his throat. I put my hand out to shush him and hunkered lower. I pulled out my camo netting before putting my backpack back on, and half wrapped it around me as I laid on the ground.

Raider had smelled something. He'd only alerted on deer when I'd asked him to track, so I was making an assumption here that his aggressive rumble only meant there was a threat nearby. I sat and waited while mosquitos buzzed around me. Ten minutes, twenty. Raider belly crawled to my side, so I pulled the netting over him as well. His coloring blended well with the undergrowth in general if he didn't move around. He made a low chuffing sound when I did that then went silent. I stroked his fur softly, willing him to be quiet, but he'd let me know when something was coming.

He tensed, his body trembling in anticipation. I strained my senses and heard something move in the brush ahead of me. I couldn't tell the distance, and if I was hunting, I would have been more upright to get a better view, but Spider's boys had been more dangerous than anything else I'd hunted. A twig snapped, and I pulled the rifle to my shoulder and sat up slightly under the netting I'd put down. A branch moved, then I saw a hand. My nerves screamed, and I put the crosshairs on the spot I expected somebody to step out in front of. I clicked the safety off, careful to keep my finger off the trigger. Raider panted, his entire body shaking.

"Shhh," I whispered, not looking up.

A man dressed in ragged clothing stepped into sight, followed by two children. All were dirty, but after watching them a moment, I realized that they'd rubbed dirt on their exposed skin, finger marks of dried mud visible. I waited as the man held the branch for them then started moving in my direction. They were quiet but had been close enough that I could hear them.

"We have to be quiet," the man whispered, still headed my way. "We don't want them to find us," he admonished one of the kids.

I let them get within twenty feet of me and clicked off the safety then slowly stood, letting the netting fall off me. One of the kids saw me first and yanked on the man's hand. I stood to my full height, the rifle at the low and ready.

"Luke—"

The man put his hand over the boy's mouth then froze in place as he saw me.

"Mister, I don't want no trouble, please," he pleaded.

"Who are you?" I asked.

"Luke," he said quietly as the kids got behind him.

He was unarmed, and now that I was upright, I could see the scratches that pushing through the brush had given him. Dried blood crusted on the tops of his hands, and he had a few scratches on his face. He was in his late forties if I had to guess, with dark hair. At one point he'd been a large man, but I could see the marks of hunger and desperation on his face. His clothing was in tatters, but he had a familiar looking radio on his belt.

"Where are you coming from, Luke?" I asked. "And tell the kids, I mean you no harm."

"How do I know that?" the man snapped. "You're with them, aren't you?"

"With who?" I asked, noting him turning slightly, getting ready to bolt.

"The KGR and the crazy survivalist group."

"I'm not with those bastards," I said softly.

Raider barked once and sat near my side, his shoulder bumping my leg, letting me know where he was.

"You're not ... who are you?"

"Westley Flagg," I told him.

Something in his body relaxed visibly, even though he shuddered.

"Oh, thank you Lord, thank you!" he said, walking forward suddenly.

Raider let out a warning growl, and the man froze, his hand outstretched.

"Go see if there's any others then come back to me, boy. I got this."

Raider whined as the man stayed frozen where he was. The two kids, boys I noted, suddenly moved forward.

"Mister Westley?" one of them asked.

"That's me," I told him.

"Miss Jessica said you had a dog like hers, said we would know you when we saw you. Is it really you?"

"It's really me," I told them.

Raider looked up at me, then back at them. "Go," I told my pup, "fetch."

Raider let out a disgusted sound and bounded off past the startled trio.

"Jessica, you've seen her? Talked to her?"

"Yes, she's back a ways with Sheriff Jackson and her mother."

"I... She's alive? She's alright?" I asked, my voice cracking with emotion.

"Why sure, she said ... say mister, are you all right?"

I sat down hard. My head swam, and I realized I was close to fainting in relief. The man closed the distance, and I set the rifle aside and wiped my face. He hunkered in front of me, though the kids kept their distance.

"We were all kidnapped by the KGR," Luke told me. "Some of us thought it was a good idea to turn the tables on our captors when their backs were turned. It ... didn't work out as we planned, but a lot of us got away. Jessica was having us move out in small groups in case the folks hunting us caught up."

I took his outstretched hand, and he pulled me to my feet and, without letting go, pulled me into a hug. "Thank you for finding us."

"I…"

"Silent Hunter, this is Girl Scout. Inbound," a radio the man had clipped to his side said, the volume so low I could barely hear it.

"Silent hunter is out of pocket," Lester's voice replied. "He's going to be damned happy to hear this. What's your ETA?"

"You should hear us coming any moment," Jessica replied. "Let the sentries know please. Part of the group is on foot, and Mom and I are rolling in captured equipment. Please, no friendly fire."

"You're Silent Hunter?" Luke asked me as Raider barked from a distance with a happy sound.

"Yeah," I said, and took the radio he'd unclipped.

"Silent Hunter copies transmission," I said, tears running down my face, "and for the record, I love you."

"Silent Hunter… I so much… I'll see you in twenty?"

"Might take me longer than that to get back. Found some wayward sheep lost in the jungle, over," I said, remembering neither of us had been saying that.

"Copy that. We're breaking radio silence, people, get organized, call in and get found. Silent Hunter, I love you too. We have a lot to talk about, but there's about to be a lot of radio chatter. We can talk when we get home. Over."

"Copy that. See you soon. Over."

Raider barked again, bounding through the grass and through the brush at a slow run.

"That'll be more of them I reckon," Luke said as we waited and listened to people from both the homestead and the incoming groups called in.

BY THE TIME LUKE, THE KIDS, AND ANOTHER SMALL group of folks I didn't recognize walked in with Raider and I, I'd heard the roar of heavy motors pass the road and then shut off. Raider kept running ahead of us, his nose to the ground. I'd taken out my radio and heard everybody coordinating, and a couple of folks from the lookouts reported they'd found the groups. I wanted to run ahead, but I didn't dare. The folks were walking behind me single file and when I got on the trail, my heart soared. It wouldn't be long now.

A FEW MOMENTS LATER, I COULD SEE TRUCKS PARKED IN the yard in front of the barn. Next to the APC we'd blown was another APC, almost an exact twin, along with a transport truck. Everyone was out in the yard. I could hear the voices from a hundred yards away. Most were happy, but there were wails of anguish. Raider didn't wait, he took off at a dead run, and two furry shapes shot past my grandma who was hugging the life out of somebody. The three dogs met in the driveway, playing and nipping at each other.

Grandma let go of the figure and pointed uphill. I saw Jessica the same moment she saw me, and we both started running. I was loaded down, but I didn't care. All thoughts and caution left me as I ran to my woman. She was smaller, lighter, and could run faster. She jumped into the air and into my arms near the top of the driveway, riding me down to the ground, laughing, crying. Then we were kissing and rolling around on the grass, both of us letting the emotions overtake us.

"That's not very hygienic," the older boy with Luke said, coming to a stop next to us.

"Says the boy with dirt smears on his face," I said, pushing my face back from Jessica's and getting my breath back that she'd knocked out of me.

THE GROUP HADN'T COME BACK empty-handed either. They'd brought a deer somebody had startled up and killed, breaking noise discipline. Jessica had wanted to chew him out for that, but everyone was happy. We had enough of the captured MREs and grains to go along with the deer that I figured we could do another large pot of stew. Venison stew with rice and whatever veggies we could find. Lester, Grandma, and Emily wanted to update me on the tasks I'd asked of them, but I only half listened, all of them smiling.

"I've got to go use the restroom and clean up," Jessica said, getting up from the chair she'd been sitting on next to me.

"Please, you stink," I said, pinching my nose and waving my other hand in her direction.

She laughed and was about to go inside, when Emily stepped in the doorway, blocking her.

"You ok?" she asked Jessica quietly.

"You know I am," Jessica said to her, obviously trying to keep her voice low.

"No, I mean about the other thing?"

"I... It's not a good time," Jessica said, shooting a glance at me.

"You almost didn't come back," Emily snapped, her smile leaving her face. "Mary and I are going to clean up after supper and head to the barn. You have that talk tonight."

"I will, but right now isn't—"

"If you don't tell him, I will." Emily was defiant, angry.

"Please, Emily, it's my—"

"Just letting you know how it is. Tonight, or tomorrow over breakfast I will."

Jessica's face turned bright red, not in embarrassment, but in anger. She put her hand up, a finger pointing, her mouth opening and closing several times. Then she grabbed her pack and pushed past the little woman. Emily stared after her a moment and then went to my chair and sat next to the three dogs that were sunning themselves on the porch.

"Is there something I need to know? You two have been keeping secrets, and it hasn't gone unnoticed."

Emily turned to me, glaring. "It's not my place to talk to you about it. Please don't push this right now."

I swore under my breath and got up, taking my pack and long gun with me. Jessica was just slamming the bathroom door as I set my pack down inside the door and leaned the rifle against the wall. I was frustrated, confused, and deeply curious. These two had suddenly been friendly, so much so that it had worried me. Now Emily was turning her fire on Jessica, and apparently Jessica had something to tell me. I was worried, and was it worse news than we'd already had?

I went to the pantry and pulled down some of the newer shine I'd made. I had a plan in place, and I was going to need booze to enact it. Linda and Sheriff Jackson were already organizing the defenses and manning them again. I'd seen her briefly, and she'd been more silent than usual, but she didn't give me any dirty looks. She'd heard about Grandpa apparently, though she didn't mention it. I think she was still coming to terms with her own loss and my part in it. I prayed someday she'd forgive me.

Grandma had some sun tea in the windowsill in a big one-gallon jar. I took that, along with two pitchers off the drying rack, before going to the pantry and getting Grandma's lemonade mix out. I couldn't do it the same way she could, but with proofed shine, I would mix about a third of shine, then the rest water, then the mix and stir it up. I did the first pitcher that way, then mixed a third of sun tea, a third of shine, a third of water, put the mix in and mixed it up.

I was still stirring the second pitcher when Emily, Mary, and Grandma came in. Grandma saw the jug of shine and the two pitchers and smiled sweetly.

"Did you forget to make some regular stuff for Miss Mary?"

"I ... yeah, I did," I admitted.

"That's ok, lemonade makes my tummy hurt, and I don't like tea," she informed us.

"You drank it for me yesterday?" Grandma asked her.

"I was being ... polite?" She looked to Emily, who put a hand up over her mouth.

"Well, missy, if you don't want any, we have plenty of water and other kinds of drink mix stuff, thanks to my grandson. You go look in the pantry and pick something out if you want it."

"Actually, I wanted to know if I could help with the deer?" she asked her mother.

I saw the three dogs take off running and went to the window. Instead of chasing chickens, they were all tumbling in the driveway. Kids cheered and laughed, pointing. More kids than we had before. I hadn't gotten all the info yet, but I would. As Jessica's group had walked into a trap, some of the prisoners the KGR had kept had staged a breakout, overpowering a couple of guards while everyone else was busy. They'd attacked the KGR's rear flank on their way out, eventually linking up with Linda and Jessica.

"I don't mind, honey—"

"Oh, Miss Jessica," she said, making me turn to see Jess had come out of the bathroom in new clothing, her hair wet. "How are you?"

"I'm doing good, sweetie, how are you?"

"I'm good. I'm glad you're home. Mister Wes is a grump when you aren't around."

"He was, was he?"

"Yeah. I'm glad you're doing good. What about the baby?"

"Baby?!" I asked as Jess' hand went to cover her stomach.

I turned to Emily, whose hand was now covering her daughter's mouth tightly. "I think we're going to go help skin a deer." They both fled as Emily whispered angrily to her daughter.

"Baby?" I asked again.

Grandma smiled and got a glass down from the cupboard and poured me a lemonade. "Cat's out of the bag," Grandma said, giving the glass to me.

"Cats? Baby?" It wasn't making sense.

"Yes, silly, Jessica is pregnant."

"You're pregnant?" I asked, setting the glass on the table.

Jessica had been looking down, but now she looked up at me and nodded.

"I guess my plans for getting you drunk and taking advantage of you are out the window," I said with a grin.

"Well, getting drunk is off the table for the next six or seven months at least," she said, a shy smile covering her face, "but I might want to take you fishing later on."

"Virgin ears!" Grandma said shrilly, her hands comically covering her ears. "No hearing aids will be used tonight!" She walked out the door.

"Really?" I asked her.

"Yes. I didn't... I mean, you're not mad?"

"I'm not mad, I'm..."

I was happy. There was light at the end of the tunnel after all. Was this why my life was so difficult? Oh Lord, now I thought about it the signs were there. I really was dumb.

"I'm so happy I feel like I could burst," I admitted.

"Let's sit, before you fall over," Jessica said, taking the chair next to me.

I sat and took a long drink from my glass. The alcohol hit my system almost immediately. Not eating much and having a virtually empty stomach will do that to you, but the old warmth that spread through me was welcome, like an old friend who showed up at just the right moment. Jessica put a hand on my shoulder and went to the sink, getting another glass and filled it from the bucket with a dipper and joined me.

"Have as much as you need," Jessica said with a smile. "There's both good and sad news."

"Our losses?" I asked her.

"About half that went out didn't come back. The group of state police took the brunt of the attack. I'm not sure how many of them got out, but I do know there's quite a few here, along with their families."

"Do we have enough supplies to feed everybody?" I asked her, thinking that the trailer of food wouldn't last long.

"No, but we've managed so far. With the munitions and APC we captured on our way out, Spider's men will think twice about coming at us."

"But they have the same stuff we do," I told her.

"True, but the trap we walked into? We gave as good as we got. We really put a hurt on them. We had to bugout when a group that had been sent to attack the homestead came back to reinforce them. The slave revolt? That was a gift from God, they put those KGR asshats in a pincher, making them give ground or fight on two fronts. It was horrible, but I think we won the day."

I poured myself another glass and sat back down, almost knocking all of it down with one gulp.

"What's the bad news?" I asked her.

"I was scared I couldn't keep this a secret from you anymore," she said, her hand on her stomach again.

"You can feel it?" I asked her.

"No, it's too early, my mom says. Heck, Emily was the first one to notice the signs. I took a test from a kit I'd found at the pharmacy on our way back to confirm things. Mom's pissed, but when isn't she?"

I smiled. "For the thousandth time, I'm sorry," I said softly.

"I know. We were all in impossible situations. I really miss my dad, miss that he's not going to be around when our little one is born, but I don't hate you for what happened."

"I didn't mean to—"

"I know you didn't," she said, "and Mom does too, in her own way. She's just ... Mom. Oh, and she's also mad because apparently you were checking her out when she was topless."

"I... No, I wasn't checking her... What?" I sputtered.

Jessica laughed. "Pick your jaw up off the table. We need to go to the communications room and see about those who are still checking in."

"Wait, this isn't everybody?"

Jessica shook her head. Before leaving the table, I poured myself a third drink. Anymore and the booze would start hitting me hard. I sipped at it. A father. I was going to be a father. A baby. My baby? Our baby! I followed Jessica out to where Grandma's big pot was being pulled out and set over the fire.

"So, Wes," Lester said, walking up, a shit-eating grin on his face, "what's the good news?"

"I'm going to be a father," I said softly.

"What's that? Couldn't hear you?" Grandma said, walking up next to him, her apron on and her can of chicken scratch in one hand.

I cupped my hands and screamed into the air, "I'm going to be a father!"

A cheer went up from everyone, and Jess' fingers dug into my arm. I turned to her, seeing her blushing deeply and kissed her. She pulled me in close as a couple wise assess went, "Oooohhhhh Ahhhh"

We broke the kiss when Raider barked happily from somewhere, and the kids started playing a game off near the garden. I sipped at my drink and hugged her hard.

"Sumbitch," Lester said and walked off, shaking his head.

"I want lots of great grandbabies," Grandma said

loudly, then leaned in to whisper, "The rope is in the top drawer, left dresser."

Jessica's blush turned even redder, but she nodded.

"Rope?" I asked her.

"So, one of us can go fishing," she whispered in my ear.

Then I remembered, and I felt my face get hot. She laughed.

5

OUR IED GUY, Jay Paulson, came up with enough materials to make the shaped charges out of copper. A crew had been tearing wiring out of houses and another who'd been an apprentice blacksmith made the castings. The homestead swelled in numbers, and tents had sprung up toward the back of the property as the barn had proved to be too small. We'd talked about finding travel trailers to park back there, but so far that hadn't been the priority.

The solar panels hadn't been enough to run the fridge, but we could run the well pump for a bit. The inverter that had been found wasn't the best, but when it worked, it worked. It was better than the hand pump, because with the swell of people, there was always a lineup at the pump and the cooking pot. Food was becoming a problem. We needed to find some more, and the garden we put in wouldn't be sufficient. Grandma had continued on with the census, and we had close to one hundred people on site at all times, with another twenty or thirty rotating through lookout points and radio contact.

I'd given up hope of ever getting Grandma's fridge running again. It was taking every solar panel and battery we had to keep the lights in the barn on, and the radios charged with the base station running all the time. In the week since Jessica's return, we'd heard nothing from the other side, other than coded phrases. They had changed frequencies and encryption codes, which Linda immediately broke again, but we didn't know what verbal code they were using. Linda had assigned somebody to keep listening to them constantly to see if they could suss out what "Ready Six, Blue Dog, Purple Three" meant. They weren't speaking in phrases.

Jessica was organizing with the new home guard and doing firearm familiarity with those who wanted and needed to learn. I'd helped out when I could, but I was beat. I'd been hunting, but game had been sparse, and my sleep was screwed up for more than a few reasons.

Linda saw me and Grandma sitting on the porch chatting and joined us, taking Grandpa's seat in the middle.

"Hi, Linda," I said softly.

"Hey. Um... You know if David was here, he'd be hauling out the shotgun and giving it a good cleaning..."

"I know," I said, nervous that she'd used her dead

38

husband's name and shotgun in the same sentence, then it hit me. "I don't think we have a preacher in the group, do we?" I asked her.

"You asking me permission to marry my daughter?"

My head swam, but I shook my head. "I was just asking—"

Grandma cracked up at that and got up suddenly. "Going to let you two hash it out."

"Now we can talk plainly," Linda said after a moment.

"I thought we already were," I said softly.

"You know, my daughter and I have no secrets," Linda countered.

"Yeah, she told me that, when she said you told her I was checking out your boobs."

Linda snorted, half a giggle escaping her lips, but she nodded. "I was teasing her."

"Do you hate me?" I asked her suddenly after a long pause.

"Do I hate you?" she repeated. "In my head or in my heart?"

"I don't ... both?" I asked her.

She took a deep breath, her hands going white as she gripped the arms of the rocking chair tightly.

"Part of me will never get over losing David," she said, without looking at me. "Other than Jessica, he was my entire life. My love, my best friend. You killed him," she said, looking at me. "Part of me does hate you for killing him."

I said nothing, my heart feeling crushed like an empty Coors can at a frat party.

"But another part of me saw the way we both were being manipulated after the fact. It's the same part that knew David should have never drawn his gun on you or your dog. He made that mistake, and it cost him his life. I know you said you weren't aiming for his head. You've apologized a thousand times, and if you do it again and make me cry, I'll break your face" –she took a deep breath, her chest hitching— "but in my heart and in my mind, most of me knows why it really happened. I just miss him so much."

Now she was crying. I reached across the table between my chair and Grandma's and grabbed her hand.

"So, can I marry your daughter as soon as we can find somebody to hitch us? I got a great deal on alcohol."

"You jackass," she said, grabbing my hand back tightly. "Yes, you can. She loves you to pieces too, you know. Oh Lord she pined for you when we moved away. She had this huge crush on you back then."

"Really? Do tell."

"Asshole," Linda said with a laugh, letting go of my hand and wiping her eyes with the other. "I got things to do. It was a good job starting the organizing you did while we were gone. I really came to talk to you about your idea you floated past Lester."

"The day you all came back? What do you think?" I asked her.

"I think it's a good idea, but I don't think you're the right one to do it," she said simply.

"No? Why not?" I asked her.

"You've got my grandbaby to raise," she said and then turned and left.

THE ARGUMENTS WERE BITTER. THE ATTACK ON KGR'S compound had driven home the point that doing things conventionally wasn't going to work. The problem was, were they thinking the same way? How do you combat guerrilla warfare when the other side is doing the same thing? Jessica, Linda, and I argued relentlessly about this. On one side, I didn't want Jessica to go because she was pregnant and most of her time in the service had been spent policing people and working with her dogs. She was good, I had no doubt, but for what I had in mind, I was at least an equal to her. I didn't want Linda to go because she was a whizz with the communications gear and code breaking, but she was also partnered up with the sheriff for organizing the defenses and training.

Whether or not they wanted to, every able-bodied adult here worked. Not for themselves, but for the whole community. People had their own belongings, don't get me wrong, but when a new fortified defensive position was being built, every adult, man, woman or kid who was old enough and big enough to help, worked. They didn't complain. Many of them knew what it'd been like in the other camp. A little digging? They were glad for the food they got because many of them hadn't had any in a while.

We were sorely lacking with people who had medical training. Duke and Carter's deaths had really thrown Linda and Jessica, but they had the basics down and so did a lot of others. Grandma knew a little bit about suturing wounds closed, but we didn't have a ton of medical supplies. We schemed on ways to find some, even going so far as sending a scouting party back into town under heavy guard, and the APC to check out the local doctors' offices and the drug store. Somebody had been there before us, and all the buildings were in disarray.

Emily and Mary had moved out to the barn, despite everyone's protests. Grandma had even offered to let them sleep in the big bed with her but was turned down. She'd been trying to spend time with Marshall as of late, and I wished them both the best of luck, but I could tell the interest was one-sided.

"What are you thinking, Grandson?" Grandma asked, joining Raider and I on our walk.

"That for once, things are going right," I said knocking on the wooden stock of the .22-250.

"Remember that idea you and Lester were talking about?"

"Knocking down the KGR's numbers?" I asked her.

"That one. You still thinking about that?"

"Yes," I said. "Though we seem to be having a feud on how many goes, and who goes."

"Did you ever wonder if it might be time to hit the other camp? The one where that Henry fella lives?"

"Actually," I said grinning, "I have."

"I saw the Saran Wrap in your backpack near the door, with some other things. What are you thinking?" she asked pointedly.

"Of making life difficult for people. I think maybe having a small team of say, three to four people, with no dogs, make the trek and put the fear of God into Henry, if we can't outright kill him right off the bat."

"Shoot him from a ways off?" she asked.

"If I can," I admitted. "I figure everybody in that entire camp carrying a gun is on Henry's side. There will be no friendlies there unless they're prisoners, and the Keggers will be easy to pick out by their gear."

"You know they've probably moved men around. It might be a huge military camp by now, with the bulk of them in that bunker they ran the Carpenters out of."

"I'm sort of planning on that," I said, an evil grin pulling my lips back, showing my teeth.

"The secret way in?" Grandma asked, an eyebrow raised.

"If I have to. Yes, at least for part of it. If I can get to the air recirculating machinery and shut it down ... even if I don't, I have an idea."

"What if Henry's holed up in that cabin?" Grandma asked.

"That's what the Saran Wrap is for." I grinned.

"If you're going to do that, why not just drop a few grenades down the fireplace and call it good?"

"I almost did that when I was with Jessica. I guess there's a chance it won't kill everybody, so I was going to stuff a scrap of rug in the fireplace, wrap the vent and chimney with the saran wrap and wait a minute to make everyone leave the cabin. Then we can pick them off from a distance so we can get away."

"Awful lot of risk going up on the roof though."

"Like I said, it was just an idea at this point. I do want to start harassing them though. If Spider switches men over to that camp, then we start at his place next. Run them so ragged that—"

Gunfire interrupted us, and I hesitated a moment, figuring out it came from the front of the property.

"Go," Grandma urged.

"I love you, Grandma. Check on Jess for me."

"She's probably in the thick of it," Grandma shot back as I started running.

"Silent Hunter on the move," I said into my mic after hitting the PTT button.

"Truck full of Keggers probing the edge," Deputy Rolston said, "not looking interested in coming any closer."

"Has the other lookout checked in?" Linda's voice cut across the chatter.

"Negative," somebody else said.

"All lookouts check in now," Linda commanded.

I ran harder. Not at the direction of the gunfire, but from the west of the house. I'd originally gone that way to provide covering fire from a distance, but if that lookout hadn't checked in...

"We're missing Ten Orange," Linda said.

She'd explained the sector clock code, or color clock code. It was a way to let people know what way you were going so you didn't get caught in friendly fire. I sucked at it, but I knew which outpost was called Ten Orange, just not the color clock code. I'd sat with them last night for a time. It'd be manned by different people during this time of day, but my blood was up from the fact they hadn't checked in. Was this a sneak attack?

"Silent Hunter moving to lookout Ten Orange," I said.

Raider barked next to me, happy to be running, unafraid of what we'd find.

"Be careful Silent," Linda's voice said, "two minutes until we can back you up."

"I'll be there in thirty secs," I said, almost panting.

I slowed down as soon as I got into the brush on the west of the house and moved north towards the Crater of Diamonds. Ten Orange was across the roadway, halfway up the hill. It was a great vantage spot with good line of sight for shooting. If they took that spot, there would be trouble.

"Taking fire at the homestead," the sheriff said as gunshots rang out ahead of me from the direction of one of our reinforced lookouts.

"Raider, stick close," I said.

I was out of breath, but not as bad as I normally would have been. I'd been in great shape when the lights had gone out, but now I seemed to have been forced into more physical work and I wasn't breathing as hard as I might have been. That, and the adrenaline dump didn't hurt.

"One minute until reinforcements, Silent," Linda's voice said in my earpiece.

"Shooters in Ten Orange," I said. "Don't send anybody out in the open. I need to find an angle."

I couldn't cross the road without being seen, but I could sneak through the brush.

"Copy that Silent, Girl Scout is with me, said to let you know if you get hurt again, she's gonna kill you."

"Copy that Little Momma."

More shots rang out.

"Little Momma?" Rolston asked.

I tuned them out as people worked to surround the truck without being seen. The shots ahead of me were coming out steadily, but no injuries were being reported on the radio. Was this a double feint? Make the team on the truck obvious, this one to draw fire and somebody come in and wipe out a team? Was it a triple feint? Was I walking into a trap of my own?

6

RAIDER and I crept through the brush, me on all fours, crawling. I'd turned the volume on the radio down so I could barely hear it but was still able to hear if my call sign was spoken. I had eyes on the defensive position we were being fired from. Whoever it was, they were making good use of our handiwork. So far, it didn't sound like any of their shots had done more than kick up dirt and hit the vehicles parked near the APCs. No sooner had I thought of that, I heard the big diesels fire up and grinned. More shots rang out and Raider whined.

I could see a rifle barrel sticking out of a gap in the logs we'd staked to make a gun port. Probably good protection against small arms fire. I aimed at the barrel, the only thing I could see, and waited. If I shot too early and missed, I risked drawing attention to the fact they were under direct fire from a different direction. They were taking halfhearted potshots. Were they there to disable the vehicles? A long rip of shots came from down the road and the gun barrel pulled back out of sight.

"Little Momma, Silent Hunter here," I said into my mic.

"Silent Hunter, you have eyes on Ten Orange?"

"I do, bad angle. I think it's a feint, same with the truck full of men just out of range."

"Wait one," Linda's voice said out of the radio.

I saw somebody leaning out of the side of the defensive position and switched my aim. The man was scanning the area I was in. I willed myself to hold still. He went stiff and stood, bringing his rifle to his shoulder in one swift move. He must have seen me. That thought went through my head as I gently squeezed the trigger. I didn't have a chance for an aimed shot at his throat or lower stomach, so I put a round right at the middle as his gun went off.

Raider yipped, biting at something on the ground as I screamed, rolling to my right, coming to half a stop next to a sapling that prevented me from getting further out of the way. I desperately pulled my gun up, seeing the man had been knocked over, and was slowly rolling over, onto his hands and knees. I worked the bolt automatically as I lined up my next shot.

Guess what else isn't armored? I thought.

I put a shot into his right hip, hearing him scream in agony.

"Raider," I called.

My dog belly crawled to me. I looked away from

the target for half a second, and saw Raider was pulling himself along with three legs, and I could see a line of blood in his fur. Rage went through my body, making adrenaline dump in copious amounts.

"Silent Hunter?" I realized I'd heard this repeated.

"Copy, Raider is dinged, one target wounded, one or two more in defensive position. Unsure if our lookouts are alive or—"

A buzz saw opened up. I'd heard the sound before and it sickened me. The wood from the position that was firing on us disintegrated, and men screamed and died. The gun itself probably only fired for a few seconds, in bursts.

"Little Momma, the APC took out 10 Orange. Will assess my dog and then move to verify. Do we have backup in case this is a double feint?"

"Told you we got this covered," Linda snarked over the radio.

"APC giving lead vehicle pursuit," Jessica's voice said from the radio.

"No, it's a trap," Linda's voice came over the radio half a heartbeat faster than I had thought to say it.

"Copy that Little Momma, sending mail anyway."

The gun opened up again. This time I could see the smoke from the shots. The APC had been put on top of the hill. I rolled over to see Raider laying by my side, his teeth digging in at something on his hind leg. I pushed his muzzle back with my left hand and felt along his flank. He was bloody, but it wasn't gushing from what I saw. Right away I felt something sharp enough to cut the pad on my thumb. I wrapped my thumb and finger around it and pulled. Raider shuddered, nipping at me, nearly drawing blood of his own as I pulled the piece loose.

"It's ok boy, I got it," I said as the big gun opened up once more.

"Target hit," Jess's voice came over radio.

"Do not follow, I repeat, do not follow. I think Silent is right, this is too easy. Sit and wait."

"FLAGG HOMESTEAD. THIS IS SPIDER KILLION SPEAKING," the voice came out of a PA speaker from a distance, "SEND OUT MARSHALL WARCASTLE AND WESTLEY FLAGG OR WE'LL LEVEL THE AREA AND KILL EVERYONE WHO DOESN'T IMMEDIATELY SURRENDER."

The big gun on the APC opened up again, and I did a double take as a second one started firing. Jess had given Spider his answer.

"Little Momma," I said into my mic, "Raider has a flesh wound, nothing major, 10 Orange appears to be down and out hard. Don't have eyes on APC's target. Will advise if more targets are seen approaching."

"Don't worry, no pursuit," Jess said over the radio. "They have anti-armor, I'm sure. No mortars and no artillery. If they want to draw us out into a trap, it's going to be an old-fashioned armor duel."

"Your target neutralized?" I asked.

"Negative, disabled maybe. Some targets took hits, but men scattered."

A motion across the street caught my attention. A

man was crawling back towards the shattered remains of the formerly reinforced position. He wasn't trying to be stealthy, he was dragging half of his body, his legs limp and unmoving, his black BDUs covered in a dark viscous wetness. I held up the piece I pulled out of Raiders leg. It looked like it was part of the copper jacket of a round. A ricochet? Was there another wound I wasn't seeing? I was worried, but I couldn't let the man across the street go and my pup didn't seem to be in any danger from the wound right now.

"You stay here boy," I said, rubbing him on top of the head.

Raider shuddered. He was in pain, but I prayed he'd hold still.

"Silent Hunter moving 10 Orange,"

"Copy," Rolston's voice said. "Do you need ground backup?"

I'd broken cover and had slung my rifle, drawing my pistol. The man was grunting, crying out in pain. I could hear him long before I saw him. Small arms fire down the road distracted me, but I tuned it out and focused on him. It was the man I'd shot in the hip. His arm and the side of his face was scarlet, where something had torn a flap of skin off the side of his temple. Bone showed through in one spot. He was leaving a trail of dark blood, but despite that, I didn't see any other holes in him. I kicked any weapons, functional or not, away from the direction he'd been crawling.

"Hold it," I said, leveling my 1911.

"Just ... do it."

His voice was shaking, and there was a tired finality to his voice. I looked in the dugout space. Three men dressed like he was had been hit by the heavy machine gun. It was ... not pleasant. Two of our lookouts were lying in a puddle, their throats cut. They must have been dead and lying flat when the big gun opened up. I turned my attention back to the man.

"Silent Hunter here, we have one prisoner. Need medics to stabilize for interrogation."

The last bit was said for his benefit. We didn't have teams of medics and interrogators.

"Confirmed. May have to wait one while sweep up team and far eyes make sure this isn't a trap that hasn't sprung yet."

"Copy," I said, then turned to the man who was panting now, his skin pale.

I touched the undamaged portion of his face; it had gone clammy.

"So, what was your objective?" I asked the man.

"I'm not talking to you," he said, his words coming out in gasps.

I rolled him so he was on his back. He let out a scream as his hips and waist turned. I'd probably just injured him worse. Didn't care. I whistled. Raider came out of the bush more or less running. I saw several backpacks had been left further up in the brush, probably to give the shooters more room in the small area.

"You got first aid kits in your packs?" I asked him.

"Sure, my IFAK is in..." his face went white for a second, his breath coming out in a hiss as he pointed.

"Raider, tear his throat out if he so much as moves."

Raider had laid down next to me, but he showed the man his teeth. I grabbed the top straps on two packs and dragged them, so I was once again facing the man. I debated things, and listened to the chatter, digging into the backpack until I found a medical kit. My eyes opened. It had syringes on top of all the medical things.

"Give me one of the morphine," the man gasped.

"What was your objective? Is there another team coming in?"

"Not going to talk to you," the man said.

"Dude, I can see part of your skull. Your friends here are dead, you're going to die slowly. If I had to guess, my shot didn't end in your hip and traveled up, hitting you somewhere that's making you drag your legs ... but wait, there's more," I said, thinking of the Sham-Wow guy, "you can still feel the pain and if I decide not to do anything but wait, you'll be screaming in agony soon, dying a horrible death. Did I mention I can see part of your skull?"

His hand went up to touch the flaps of skin hanging down off the left side of his face. A sob came out and I hated being so cruel. I pulled out some anti-septic and called Raider to me. The man watched as I treated the line that had been cut through his fur and skin, ending where I'd pulled out the fragment. My hands still had my dog's blood on them.

"The pain ... it's..."

"Bad, and you're going to either die in extreme

agony, me keeping you alive as long as possible, unless you tell me about the plan here."

The man cursed under his breath. He was trembling and shaking. Despite my words, I think the shock was going to kill him soon.

"Little Momma moving Ten Orange," I heard over the radio.

"Silent Hunter copies," I said.

"Reinforcements?" The man asked with a grimace.

"No, just my mother in law. She doesn't like me very much, but she really hates you guys."

"You think you have everything figured out, don't you?" he sneered.

"Your PMC group rolls in and hooks up with a survivalist group. You kill those in the group who wouldn't go along with your plans. I'm guessing you want Wes to manufacture drugs, alcohol, bombs. You want the Marshall kid to use as leverage over Lance, though I still haven't figured out why you still need him."

"You don't even know? Do you?" He chuckled.

"What's to know, big guy?" I asked him, dropping the gauze I'd used to dress Raider's wound and pulled out a syringe labeled 'morphine'.

"I..." he licked his lips, his eyes never leaving the syringe, "One of those will work. Two or three would kill me. I don't want to..." he gasped and shuddered again, his words trailing off.

"Fill me in, or when Linda gets here, she's going to make it worse."

"Ok, ok, the shot first," he was panting, his skin color was going grey.

"Westley?" Linda called from behind me.

"You're him?" The man asked, surprised.

"Oh yuck. Looks like hamburger helper gone wrong," Linda said. "Has he talked?"

"Nope, says he won't unless I give him some morphine."

"You search him?" Linda asked, her carbine covering him.

"Not yet, just chit-chatting. Raider caught part of a copper jacket somehow. Figured I'd fix my dog up before I gave this Kegger dog anything. Let him sweat, bleed and sit in pain. My shot spined him, but it didn't cut off pain like a broken back would, for some reason."

"Oh goodie," Linda said, handing me her carbine and pulling a knife.

I slung her gun next to my other one and kept my pistol pointed at the man's chest. Linda pulled things out of his vest, though I didn't see any grenades or spare guns. Just magazines, cable ties, a lighter and a small leather pocket-sized journal. He started to complain, but Linda held the knife under his chin. She handed the journal to me. I slid it into my pocket, being careful not to poke myself, though I still had the cap on the syringe. Then she checked his ankles and pockets, throwing things as far as she could from him.

"What was your mission?" She asked, the blade of the knife still on his throat, the tip just under his chin.

"Do it, I'll never walk again anyways," he said.

"You want the syringe? If you have enough, I'll let you float away, or give you a quick painless death with a shot to the head if you talk."

"Need something. Pain is making it hard..."

Linda walked over to the open kit, but I motioned to her. She saw the syringe and took it. She pulled the cap off with her teeth and pushed the plunger, making a small amount of liquid squirt up.

"If he moves, kill him."

Raider growled low and made a false start for the man, making him flinch.

"I was talking to your dad," Linda said to Raider, "but maybe if he doesn't talk, I'll let you have a few bites."

"You wouldn't..." the man gasped.

"Why not? It isn't the first or the last time this guy has taken it personally when somebody is attacking us."

"That's the dog that got Henry?" he asked, fear showing in his eyes.

"For starters. He also got one of Lance's boys and killed a couple of the traitors when we broke out of the compound."

The man shuddered and I realized that Linda had figured out the man's phobia long before I had. Now, she was playing him like a fiddle.

"Raider, come," she patted her leg.

7

THE POTSHOTS from the westernmost position were meant to draw us out, and the truck full of cannon fodder had been used to see if the KGRs could draw out the APC into a deadly crossfire. They hadn't counted on my girlfriend being warned, and a damned decent heavy machine gunner. They had one of their remaining armored units back a mile or more waiting with DU rounds and some anti-tank mines. They hadn't counted on Jess killing the truck from afar, they had counted on her chasing it. The truck hadn't meant to get so close, but they'd used men they'd captured or converted to man it. Not professionals. Cannon fodder.

We waited what felt like an hour to confirm the man's story. He wavered in and out of consciousness.

"Are you... Did they...?"

"One last question, was Spider really here?" I asked the man.

"No, radio hooked up to PA," the man gasped, "please, you promised."

"Give me the bag," Linda said.

"Just give him the one. When he's mellow, I'll shoot him."

"Naw, I was going to give him a shot of adrenaline to wake him up first, let him suffer and sweat some more, then give him the morphine. I've never given both before. I wonder if he'll quit breathing while his heart explodes?"

"Now you're being mean," I teased.

"You better be nice to my daughter; this guy hasn't really made me mad. Mess with my baby, and I'll end you," she punctuated that by pointing at me with the knife.

"You both..." the man said, having no more moisture in his body to sweat, though he looked like he was slicked with it, "are crazy."

"I don't like that word," Linda said pulling out another syringe and laying it against the other one she'd prepped on top of a log.

"Silent Hunter, status update?" Jess's voice came in over the radio.

"Still interrogating the prisoner. Hey, are your dogs hungry? I know Raider hasn't had real food in a while. Think Diesel would like some live meat?"

"Stop, stop," the man pleaded, but Linda got the second syringe's cap off and jabbed it in his shoulder.

He let out a cry, but he didn't have the strength or

volume to really do it justice as she pushed the plunger down hard.

"Now the fun starts," she said, capping it and tossing it to me.

It was a syringe full of saline solution, probably to clean out PICC lines or whatever they were called.

"I thought you were going to hit him with adrenaline. What's this ... phenobarbital?"

"What? I gave him speed by accident. Shit. Time for the adrenaline. Sorry buddy, the pheno will probably hurt worse than the adrenaline, but I did promise you the one-two. Anything else you want to tell us?" She grabbed another syringe out and took off the cap.

"You didn't wipe his arm down first. Not very hygienic, Mrs. Carpenter," I opined.

"I've got malpractice insurance," she snarked back.

I heard voices coming up behind us and spared a glance. Emily was loaded down with her monstrous BFR on her hip, her lever gun over her back. Diesel walked at her side. On her other side was Jessica, who held a pistol that was almost the twin of mine out at the low and ready. Yaeger was on her other side. Sheriff Jackson, Deputy Rolston and two other men fell in behind them, one of them Curt Gutheries, the other a new guy. The man saw me looking at reinforcements and took a peek for himself.

"What is ... that?" he wasn't strong enough to point, but his gaze was locked on Diesel.

"He's a mutant zombie dog hybrid. Really good to have in a fight, but the pig is always hungry. What do you think we've been doing with the bodies of your men we kill? No room to bury them all."

Jessica grinned wickedly and muttered something in German. Diesel wagged his stubby tail, then ran to the downed man, sniffing at his pant legs, then up in the man's ruined face. Jess barked another guttural command and Diesel went stiff, a growl coming out of his lips. I don't know how badly it scared the man, but seeing this big pup go all aggro on command had me ready to pee a little myself. He was shuddering almost uncontrollably. Probably from as much fear, as it was the shock killing him.

"I told you everything I know," the man insisted. "Please call him off, please." His gasping voice was desperate.

"Diesel, come," Emily called.

The big guy backed up a few steps and sat down but didn't listen to Emily entirely.

"Who are you being re-supplied by, and are there more reinforcements coming to your camps?"

"Resupply? Spider and Henry had most of the supplies already bought and stockpiled. Got truck-loads of things as a payment from some African warlords. Guns, ammo. Had to buy the APCs with diamonds..." he was talking fast now.

"Keep talking, I'll give you a shot to slow you down and make the pain go away," Linda cooed, picking up the morphine syringe.

"He... I... worked with him in Kenya and a few other places. Always shipped toys home by freighter.

KGR has its own truckers, fuel depots ... a big contract with the government around here—"

"What kind of contract?" I asked him.

"Something with DHS and FEMA," he panted. "Please, I don't know much, I'm just a gunner."

"Any other survivors?" I asked Jessica, smelling something burning in the distance.

"We've got three more. One of them ate a bullet from a backup gun we didn't find fast enough. Other two are singing like canaries."

"Good, so you don't need me. Please?"

"Diesel, Yaeger and Raider," I called.

All three dogs walked together and sat in a semi-circle around us.

"If he moves, he's all yours."

Diesel was drooling and the timing was perfect, he licked his chops and then let his tongue hang out to pant, a doggie grin that had way too many teeth.

"Tell me what you know about the contract," she said, jabbing the needle in and depressing it partially.

The man watched, not even flinching as he got the injection. He took a deep breath. Then another. I did a slow count and when I got to fifteen, I spoke up.

"Diesel? You hungry buddy?"

Woof!

The ground didn't quite shake with that reply, but it startled the man enough that he flinched. He looked at me in panic, but I could see his eyes glazing over.

"Tell us about the contract with DHS and FEMA," I said, "and if Linda doesn't give you the other half of that shot, I will. If you don't talk to us ... well, you can see my buddy here is hungry."

A streamer of drool hung from the side of Diesel's jaw.

"Listen, all, I know ... Spider did it to get intel on where the government stashes were. He's been saying for years that something is gonna happen. Real Dooms Day Prepper stuff. I thought he was nuts because I know what he has stashed..." his words were starting to slur, but he weakly held a hand up to me, "My journal. Picture. My daughter."

I pulled it out of my pocket and flipped it open. A pretty girl in her late teens was posed in front of a sign that said 'Welcome to LA'. I pulled it out and handed it to him. He looked at it, a small smile touching his features. I took the syringe from Linda and jabbed the rest in.

"Promise me, you won't tell Jenny?" He was staring at the picture.

"I won't," I told him.

"If you see her, tell her I'm sorry I didn't save her mom—"

BAM!

The thunderclap of Emily's revolver startled all of us more than the blood spray.

"One of his shots almost got Mary," Emily snarled.

Big scary Diesel looked at the petite woman and shuddered, then walked in front of Jess and sat at her feet.

"I really hope you do have some more prisoners," I told Jess. "Seems this one's done talking."

"What? You're pissed at me?" Emily yelled at my back.

"No, it's just that ... you've been awful quick to decide when somebody we're talking to dies."

"But you said—"

"Easy short stuff," Linda growled, "It's just an observation, not an attack."

"I don't ... I'm just trying..." she stamped her foot and then spun and turned around.

I waited half a heartbeat and pulled out my earwig and unplugged it, turning my radio up. Scouts were checking in. The men who had fled the blown truck had reached the trap area. They couldn't get close without being discovered, so they decided to wait and watch.

"We going to have to watch her." Linda said after a long pause.

"Emily? If anything came anywhere close to her daughter, I'd say she was justified," I said quietly.

"You would take her side, wouldn't you?" Jessica asked sharply.

"What?" I asked her.

"It's just ... I can't even ... Yaeger, Diesel, come." Jessica spun and walked away, stomping in the same direction Emily had gone.

"Did I miss something?" I asked Linda.

"It's just ... Jessica is a patient woman, even forgiving. More so than I am. Emily doesn't exactly hide her feelings for you. You taking on a somewhat parental role in Mary's life—"

"Wait, I'm what?" I said surprised.

"Well, that's how it looks to people," Linda said, "and I know you're fond of the girl, but who isn't? She's a cute kid. But you and Jessica are about to have a family of your own."

She was going through the backpacks and stripping gear and tossing it to the men who'd accompanied the dogs and ladies. They were making trips back to the barn, coming and going, some more squeamish than others. I was going through the medical kits. They were surprisingly well equipped. If Spider was sending his cannon fodder out with good stuff... My mind reeled. Antibiotics, morphine, the adrenaline that Linda had promised to use on the dead man but had faked it and something in a vial I didn't recognize the name of.

"It's a sedative, knocks people out. This was a grab and snatch team, maybe?" Linda said, "Probably a couple of them had advanced medical training."

"But they threw these men's lives away," I told her.

"Maybe it was a quadruple feint?"

I ignored that. "So, what do I do? You know I love your daughter. I want to marry her, but I can't help how Emily feels and I don't want to hurt that little girl's feelings. I'm the one who killed her father." The last part was almost whispered.

"Done a lot of that," she said acidly, then winced when she saw the expression on my face.

"Sorry, I'm still ... all of this. My daughter pregnant, my husband dead... You're hard to get along with, but you're impossible to truly hate. You figure this shit out. It's your job as head of the house now."

The men shifted from foot to foot. Rolston and the Sheriff took over for Linda, who had turned, wiping her bloodied hands on her pants, then she took her carbine from me and walked off. "I've got other shit I have to do."

I looked up at Rolston, who was looking anywhere but at me. Sheriff Jackson was likewise.

"Guys, clue a kid in, would you?" I asked them.

"Remember that time I said one wants to protect you, one wants to scratch your eyes out and one wants to kill you?"

"Yeah?" I asked Rolston.

"I think the roles flipped again today. A pregnant fiancé with your other lady love switching from house to barn and back and forth? Dude..."

"I'm not ... it's not like that. And I haven't proposed yet, so don't ruin my surprise."

"Sure," Jackson said, his hands deep in the bloodied gear Linda had stripped to salvage but hadn't sorted through.

"You know what guys? Eat shit." I stood up. "Raider, come."

"You could always propose to both, live like those fellas on TV with four wives and eighty children?" This was from one of the State Policemen, Elias, that had come to live at the homestead.

"I can't even keep one lady happy; I piss her mom off all the time, and nothing I do will ever be good enough," I raved.

"Sounds like you've been married before," Rolston said with a snicker.

I flipped them the bird to a chorus of snickers and 'good luck' thrown into the mixture. I had to get my dog back to the house and let Grandma look at him. He'd remained in good spirits and was moving around now without a limp, though I knew it hurt. We'd have to clean it out again and see if he needed a stitch or two.

8

THE JOURNAL WAS HALF DIARY, half list of supplies. I found that out by flipping through the pages, and an address towards the back stood out. It was the area we'd found the stashed food in the tumbled down barn. I tried to put that together with the other address, on a mental map. I needed a county map, and I knew where one was. Problem with that, it was in the barn, and I was being given the silent treatment. By all three ladies. Mary didn't hate me, that was something.

She interrupted my thoughts, coming into the house for breakfast like nothing was wrong.

"Hey there," Grandma said, "how did you sleep?"

"Hi Grandma, Hi Mister Wes. I didn't sleep too well. My mom still has bad dreams."

"Why aren't you sleeping in your own bed out there?" Grandma asked her.

"Miss Jessica slept on my bed last night," Mary said without any annoyance.

"Now why would she do that?" Grandma asked, but she was looking at me.

"I think she's mad that Mister Wes... I don't remember exactly. Something he said to her?"

I sighed and got up to pour coffee. "You want something to drink, sprout?"

"Is it true you're acting like you're my daddy?"

I dropped the mug, and it shattered in the sink. I jumped back so the shards wouldn't hit my bare feet and then searched for Raider. He wasn't under the table, but on my spot on the couch. He cocked his head to the side as if to ask what sort of dumbassery I was up to.

"Let me get the broom. You get the big chunks gathered, but don't walk anywhere. Going to get glass in the bottom of your feet if you do."

I nodded, answering Grandma without turning and started stacking big chunks into the remnants of the mug. Not much had exploded and flown out of the sink but there was some and ceramic was wicked sharp.

"Sorry, did I scare you?" Mary asked in a little voice.

"Just surprised me," I told her, turning in place so I could see her, "but you'd never scare me, pipsqueak."

"Before Momma went to bed, her and Miss Jessica were out back arguing. I could hear the yelling right up until the cop guys in the tents yelled at them to knock it off."

This was not good.

"Did they, I dunno, apologize to each other?" I

asked as Grandma, a dervish of efficiency, came back with broom and dustpan and started sweeping around my legs.

"No, Momma told Miss Jessica she didn't care and that she should talk to you and not her."

"About what though?" I asked.

"I don't know. I'm only six, I'm not a mind reader. Sheesh."

I grinned and lifted the leg Grandma whacked so she could sweep under it. Then I waited and did the other until it was safe to move. I carried the broken shards and the remainder of the mug to the trash bin and dropped it down.

"Well, if you were a mind reader, what would I be thinking?"

"Mister Wes, I don't want to know." She let out a dramatic sigh. "Momma said nobody can figure you out. I figure if I ever did, would I want to know if I really knew?"

I didn't understand that.

"Do you think either of them will talk to me?" I asked her seriously.

"Westley, quit pumping the girl for information!" Grandma admonished, dumping the dustpan in the trash, then walking both back to the pantry.

"Sorry. You want eggs? Some taters and corn-bread?" I'd cooked earlier and still had half a pan full.

I'd forgotten that Grandpa hadn't been around and made too much. It pained me, every little reminder of him. Of how he'd died in Grandma's arms, how the bullets had nearly cut him in half. I'd been too late to say my final goodbye.

"Yes please," she said.

Grandma came back to the table and sat down. I scooped a generous portion of everything onto a plate and set it in front of her, then got the percolator from the cooler side of the cooktop on the stove and poured Grandma and I warmups.

"Thank you," she said in between mouthfuls.

"You got to fix this," Grandma said, pointing at me with the hand holding the coffee cup.

"How?" I asked her. "When I'm not even sure what I did wrong?"

"You love too much," Mary said, in between bites.

"What's that dear?" Grandma asked her.

"He's too nice to people. Everybody knows my mom likes him, and Miss Jess likes him, and I like him and he's always so helpful with everyone. Even Marshall likes him!" The last two was said with such innocence that I had to fight a snicker, but the dirt was coming out. It was getting good.

"So, Miss Jess thinks she has to fight for my Grandson's affections?" Grandma asked her gently.

"I don't think nobody wants to fight Miss Jess, she's rougher than any of the boys I know."

This time I did snort, wearing a slap to the back of my head just as I was getting a drink of now warmed coffee, spilling it on the table.

"Grandma—"

"Don't you 'Grandma' me Wes, get the cloth."

I put the cup down, rubbing the back of my head and checking my shirt to see if I'd spilled any on me. Not that it'd matter much. I got the washcloth from the sink and used the dipper to pour water over it to wet it and went back to the table, wiping up my mess.

"So, here's the deal," Grandma told Mary. "It sounds like your Mother and Jess are arguing over whether or not my Westley here has the cooties."

"Wait, I thought he was immune? I might catch them from him. Ewwwwwwwwwwwwwwwwwwwwwwww!"

I had to get out of here.

"Don't you go nowhere. Sit your butt back down." Grandma pointed to my spot. I'd been planning on getting another coffee cup and sitting next to Raider, and out of range of her back-of-the-head slap. So, I did the manly thing. I opened my mouth, closed it again, and sat back down.

"I don't have cooties," I told Mary. "But I will admit, I don't know why I made the ladies mad at me or each other. I'm not going to even guess."

I took a sip of caffeine so I could avoid speaking more.

"It's about sex, isn't it? Grownups always fight about sex!"

I spit my coffee and started choking. Grandma wasn't amused as I hacked and coughed. With tear-filled eyes, I made my way to the sink and leaned over it, trying to clear my lungs. Grandma smacked my backside, so I reached in the sink and handed back the washcloth. By the time I'd caught my breath, both Grandma and Mary were solemn faced, but broke out into grins. They'd been whispering.

"What?" I asked them both.

"Nothing," Mary said a little too quickly.

I ignored them both and stomped dramatically (but in a manly fashion) to the couch and sat at the far end, patting my leg. Raider crawled over and laid across my legs and stretched out so I could rub his stomach. I did, but I also checked out the cut. It hadn't needed stitches and the piece I'd pulled out hadn't gone very deep. Grandma had cleaned it out again and when Raider wouldn't quit licking it, she told him she was going to get him fixed if he didn't quit it. Apparently, my dog was smarter than I was, because he quit digging at a sore spot, something I seemed unable to do. Metaphorically speaking.

THE BARN WAS A HIVE OF ACTIVITY, BUT IT WAS ALMOST all talking was being done in hushed voices. The beds were being used in shifts. The crew that stayed up late defending the place were now either in the beds sleeping, or out back in the tents with earplugs in. The very front where the radio was, was the only place where noise wasn't a concern. That's where I found Linda.

"Coward. Come slinking in here now of all times?"

"What do you mean? Jess didn't come inside last

night, I figured she wanted to be left alone so I left her alone."

"She might have acted like that, but you should have come out here last night and talked to her," Linda said half listening with a headset on her head, one ear covered.

"Do relationships come with an instruction manual?" I asked her, a note of exasperation in my voice.

"Nope, but you should have this all figured out by now. My daughter is the least girlish girly girl you're ever going to meet, and she puts up with a lot with you."

I flopped down on the bench next to her, pulling out the journal and handing it to her. She looked at me, puzzled, and examined the exterior. It was leather bound, slightly bigger than a deck of playing cards, with a clasp to hold the cover closed. She looked up at me for a moment, then thumbed open the clasp. I pointed to a scrap of paper I stuck in and she flipped to the page.

"Look at that," I said, pointing to the address.

"What's this mean?" she asked me puzzled. "I'm busy here, so just give me the short version."

"That's the address we found the stashed food," I told her. "There's a dozen addresses in his notebook alone, along with personal stuff about his daughter, where to find his will, and his writings about the KGR that's interesting, but not helpful."

"Wait, more supply drops?"

"You read it. I'm headed out. If the ladies don't want

to talk to me, they don't have to. They want space away from me, so be it."

"You're a whole lot of sour grapes this morning. What got you so riled up?"

"I ... it's just ... Mary. She overheard Jess and Emily arguing yesterday. Seems to think it has something to do with sex."

Linda dropped the book, then quickly tried to pick it up. The headphones pulled tight and when the plug came out of the radio, the already coiled wire snapped at her, smacking her in the back of the head. She let out a surprised yelp and rubbed the spot the jack had hit.

"Crap! Now I know what it feels to be like you when your Grandma whacks you. Where are you going anyways?"

"Bye," I said waving.

I had a radio on my belt, which was becoming normal. I didn't have a vest like a lot of folks here did. Instead I dressed as my normal: boots, jeans, a plaid shirt open in the front a couple of buttons, though it was starting to get chilly as fall was finally kicking in. I had my holstered .45, two spare magazines and my pocketknife. I had to double check my pockets. I eyed the first stall that used to be Grandpa's powder room and detoured that way.

Lester was inside. Several rifles had been broken down and the parts were on a bench that hadn't been in there before. Pegs had been driven into the wall as weapons and supplies were hung. I did a slow circle and let out a whistle. This place was set up like a gun shop, or armory. Which in a way, I guess it was. With our new armorer.

"Lester," I said quietly, not wanting to startle the man who had small parts laid out on the table.

"Wes?" he said, turning. "Oh, good to see you. How are you and your Grandma doing?"

"Pretty good. You look like you're keeping pretty busy," I said, looking around.

Guns and rifles of all types were in here, but the majority were ones that had been captured, if I had to guess. Wooden crates were stacked across one wall, with letters stamped in green. Les saw my look and where I was looking, then turned back at me and motioned me over.

"This was with the supplies that Linda captured along with that APC."

"I'm still not clear how they captured one," I told him.

"It wasn't manned at the time and a couple fellas in the group had used something similar to it back in the day. The APCs we have here; the wrecked one we're stripping, and the good ones are both Grizzly LAVs. Old ones."

"The guy Linda and I interrogated said Spider had bought tons of stuff on the black market in Africa."

"Makes sense, the Canadians sold a ton of these off when they became obsolete or too expensive to upgrade."

"I thought they'd be enclosed in the top," I said, confused.

"Some are, some aren't. About a thousand ways to configure these things. You aren't here about taking that out for a drive, are you?"

"No, no," I assured him, "I was wondering if you'd had a chance to check out my M4 and the Ammunit-"

"I didn't forget! Right over here," he said, motioning to one of the longer barreled guns hanging on the wall.

"Wow," I said softly as he took it down and handed it to me.

The barrel was significantly longer than it had been, and with the suppressor, I bet it added a good foot or more to the length.

"I had to change the upper out. Had a problem with your..." he told me things he did that I didn't understand. It wasn't that I didn't want to learn, but he was so fast that most of it flew right over my head. The bottom line was he had an upper with a barrel on it, so he could mount the suppressor on easily. It even had glass on it.

"Has it been sighted in?" I asked him.

"Nope. Figured I'd let you do that. That way you can get a feel for where it hits. I've got the suppressor on it right now, but if you're not going to be using it, twist it off and store it and shoot regular ammo. That thing's a bit of pain to clean out, but it's a really good unit. Quiet too!"

"You tried it?" I asked him.

"You didn't hear it?" he asked me grinning.

"Um... no," I told him, feeling like a high school kid whose parent just threw him the keys to a Ferrari and a $100 bill for beer money.

"Well then, you'll have to try it out and let me know what you think. Match grade barrel on an Aero Precision upper. The bolt carrier group—"

"Les, I need the ammo," I said, my mind unable to absorb everything he was telling me.

"Oh yeah, right." He went to the steel wire shelving that had been put up since the last time I was there and pulled down a cardboard box of ammo.

"That's it?" I asked him looking inside.

"That's a hundred rounds of hand loaded, subsonics—"

"So, I don't want to use a lot of this?"

"Only when you want to be quiet. Your regular ammo is too fast for the suppressor to do much for you. These are quiet boy, but you really need to use this ammo when you're wanting to take down game silently."

"It weighs more than my bolt gun," I said, though I did like the balance of things.

"Yeah, but your bolt gun holds five rounds and the ammunition is going to be hard to reload unless I find more casings for it. I'm guessing your grandpa had reloaded some of that brass more than a couple of times."

"I'm ... yeah, I'm sure you're right."

"So now you have something else to try. I figure at

the lower velocity, the subsonic are going to shoot lower than zero for regular NATO ammo. Up to you where you want to put this scope at. Depends on what think you're going to be shooting more of."

"Thank you," I said, taking the box in my hands and slinging the rifle over my shoulder.

"Les, you playing with those guns again?" An older widower asked him, somebody who'd come in with the second group, named Melinda.

"Yes ma'am. Wes, if you'll excuse me, I have to lock up here. Me and this young lady have a walk to take."

He dropped a wink at me as the gal just smiled sweetly. Then I got it. Ugggg. Everything was about sex. The kid was right. It was official, I was grossed out.

"Later," I called, heading back to the house.

9

THE SCOPE MUST HAVE BEEN USED with this upper and
barrel before. I only had to adjust it slightly to hit
bullseye. I knew what I could do with Grandpa's tack
drivers, well, mine now... But this was right up there,
on par or better. The subsonic ammunition and
suppressor surprised me. I knew it wasn't going to be
whisper quiet, but Lester had been right about how it
shot. I went through ten rounds with it. Three to
confirm where the zero point was, and the rest to gauge
how quiet the gun actually was. Anybody more than
thirty feet away would probably hear the clacking of
the action, but the actual shot itself was a little louder,
but ... muffled. It was hard to explain.

Lester had shown me how to clean the suppressor
after that. When I had asked where Emily, Mary and
Jessica had gone, Linda had ignored me. Still mad at
me too. Grandma had fixed me a lunch to go, so after I
washed up, I got my gun belt with the dump pouches. I

filled three magazines with the hand loads and dug around in the junk drawer in the kitchen. I found the electrical tape I'd been looking for right off. It was a light blue for some reason. I taped the three magazines with the hand loads so I could find them in a hurry and loaded one in the mag well.

"You going head hunting?" Grandma asked.

"I'm going to walk. Can I leave Raider here with you? I know he'll want to come, but I don't want his leg to get infected."

"I'll keep the furry beast occupied," Grandma said. "I'm going to be making some venison and cornbread later on, so don't be out too late."

"I don't plan on it. Got a new toy to play with, got half the ladies here mad at me, need to walk and clear my head some."

"Girl problems," Grandma said with a nod.

"Apparently. Both Jessica and Emily aren't around either, oddly enough."

"Going to go look for them?" Grandma asked.

"No, I think I'm headed east, towards Emily's family's old farm. Check it out. Spider's men have probably cleared out of that area for good, but maybe I can find trace of the two families that didn't get caught up."

"I thought Emily didn't cotton to them much?" Grandma asked an eyebrow raised. "Trying to get rid of her?"

I chuckled. "Grandma, for better or worse, for richer or poorer..."

Grandma cackled and rubbed her hands together. "Let Jess hear that, and your ass is grass."

"I was kidding, hey, you know I was kidding, right?"

"You are so dead meat," Grandma said grabbing her apron and the bucket of scratch and heading out the door.

"Grandma, I was kidding!"

NOT QUITE EVERYONE OBJECTED WHEN I GOT ON MY BIKE, but most of them did. I put in my earwig, turned on my radio, and shouldered my backpack and rifle. I took off slowly, hating to hear Raider whining and barking as I left. He loved to run on the road beside me, but I didn't want him to today. I needed to figure things out.

Was I as much of an open book as Emily was?

I flat out loved Jessica, I was certain of that. I knew how Emily felt about me, but I wasn't sure how I felt about her. There was definitely chemistry that went both ways. Emily and Jessica had both cared for me when I was down and out, almost dead. Despite that, it was Emily who I'd woken up and seen. Jessica had been busy with her group, family stuff. Emily could have left at that point and avoided her daughter later getting shot, but she didn't want to leave me.

Every time we got close, I felt my chest tighten slightly. When she'd pulled her shirt up and I'd rubbed the scars on her side, I hadn't meant that to be such an intimate moment. I'd been more horrified by the abuse

81

she'd endured and had acted without thinking. And we'd been close. So close we'd slept in the same bed, same couch, same blankets on more than one occasion.

I'd never once been inappropriate with her, but when we'd been working on the solar panels, she'd gotten close to me again, pressed herself against me. I remembered the way her breath tickled the back of my neck, how she'd raked her nails across my chest. It had all been a tease and a goodbye of her fantasy I suppose. Was that why Jessica accused me of taking Emily's side? Did she think something happened?

I pondered that, and figured out the Mary portion of why it upset Jessica right off. If I had a close or closer bond with Mary since I'd known her longer, and she was already past the baby stuff, diapers, burps, puke ... would I feel the same way about our baby? At least I think I had it right. Thinking about this stuff made my head hurt.

I slowed my bike when I got to where I had stopped the first time. Pushing it into the weeds, I covered it up the best I could. I'd gone on alone when I could have driven with a team, but I didn't want a team, I wanted to do what I'd always done. Lone wolf it. I was in my element. I took my binoculars out of my pack and hung the strap around my neck and made sure I could get to my camo netting in a hurry, and then started my stalk.

I wasn't stalking prey, I wasn't hunting, but I was wary the same way I was when I'd poached when I had been younger. I listened to the sounds of the wildlife, the birds, the trees. Nothing was indicating anything wrong, but I slowed down, the hairs on the back of my neck starting to stand up. Something wasn't right, and I didn't know what it was. By the time I got close enough to get a glimpse of the farm, I was crawling. What I saw both surprised me - and didn't.

Men and women were working the field, and it wasn't just a couple of them. It looked to me to be a small army. Areas that hadn't grown crops were being turned over by hand with a shovel. I had to get out of here, but I needed to get more info. I was slowly glassing the area, when I stopped dead. There was a man moving amongst the workers with a shotgun. I recognized his friend as well, who was calling out orders. Lance.

I kept a mental eye on him and scanned the faces of the workers. None of them were happy, many looked downright malnourished. What I didn't see though was what made me worry, and in my mind, put the nail in the coffin of Lance. There were no young ladies or kids to be seen. Who had been the guy they were going to trade them for? With some preparation I might be able to do something, but now I was alone. I knew for sure there were two or three gunmen overseeing the fields being tended and I didn't see any of the ladies or kids who'd fled from here, Emily's family.

I slowly made my way back to my bike, being even more careful than I had been going in. Mid-day had turned to early evening. The sun was still up, but it wasn't shining on me as brightly as it had been. At least now I knew why they were keeping Lance around. As a local, he'd known who had what planted where. If he'd been supplying booze and drugs, he'd know who he could get to do his dirty work, and he must have made his deal with Spider, thinking he'd had the whip hand. He hadn't, and now he was still doing the same thing, but with the threat of Marshall being harmed. Did he know we had him? Would that be a relief?

"Silent Hunter, this is Girl Scout," Jess said into my earpiece.

"Silent Hunter here," I whispered. "I'm getting out of dodge, can't talk." I prayed my voice didn't carry, even though it was whispered.

I was uncovering my bike when she spoke again.

"Do you have eyes on target group? If yes, one click, no is two clicks."

I hit the PTT button once.

"Are you near where you told Grandma?"

One click.

"KGR?"

I hesitated and then did one click, then two clicks.

"Are you in a safe location?"

One click.

"Stay put, we can get a team there in ten minutes."

Two clicks.

"Dammit Silent."

Two clicks.

Somebody had told her the frequency I was going to be monitoring, must have been Linda. A motor fired up nearby and I dropped to the grass, pulling my camo netting out and over me and the bike. Being fall, the grass and brush had grown taller than when I'd first been here, but the leaves were turning, not falling yet. I could blend in, but I didn't want to risk discovery. I didn't know who was coming and what their intentions were. Voices drifted to me from upwind, from the direction of the farm.

"Did you send a team?" I asked quietly into my radio.

"No," Jess said immediately.

"I think you might have to, after all. Standby."

"Loading up," Linda said instead of Jess. "Standby Silent. No more transmissions. They might be trying to DF our transmissions."

One click.

Was this a trap? Had I made myself bait to draw us away from our defenses? Would this be how the new life was? Always hunted, always under surveillance. I had been sure nothing had happened here, and I'd been planning on at least taking a cursory look for Emily's family members. More than that though, I wanted to get away from the homestead for a bit. Stupid. I'd been stupid. Again.

"Can you signal us when we're close?" Jess asked into the radio.

I hesitated, then pressed the button.

TEN MINUTES SEEMED TO LAST AN HOUR OR LONGER. I got into a comfortable position and listened to the motor rise and fall until I heard a new sound. Another motor approaching from the homestead. I heard a shout on the wind and strained to hear, but the words were lost to me. I settled in to wait. For good or bad, I was committed now, and so were a truckload of people. I didn't have as long to wait as I thought. It only felt like two hours but was probably five minutes all told.

Linda's truck came into view up the hill, coming down the road to the west of me. Three shapes stood up over the bed of the truck and I could see two figures in the cab. I started pressing the button.

Click click click click click.

The truck came to a stop about twenty feet behind my position on the roadway. I looked up the road and saw nothing. I hit the button again for good measure, then drew up, pulling the camo netting off of me. There were a few startled exclamations from the bed of the truck, but Sheriff Jackson put his hand out to the man who'd turned his rifle in my direction. I slung my rifle in a hurry and picked my bike up with one hand and dragged the camo netting with the other as I made my way at full speed to the truck. Jess was in the driver's seat, Emily in the passenger seat. The Sheriff, Deputy Rolston and Curt Gutheries were in the bed. I handed my bike up, and Rolston just swung it in as Sheriff Jackson took the netting.

I'd put my foot on the rear tire when someone grabbed the strap on my pack and bodily hauled me into the truck. I hit face first, my nose smarting. Somebody hit the top of the cab and the truck spun around in a way that should have given me whiplash. Through the open middle window, I heard Emily radioing back to the homestead. She must have been on a different frequency than I was, because I didn't hear the reply in my earpiece. I rolled onto my side and got a hand on the bed of the truck and pulled myself into a sitting position.

"What's going on?" I asked the guys who were staring at things behind us.

"Linda was right, they've been DF'ing our transmissions. That electrical engineer guy broke their codes, or at least some of them." Curt was speaking, but not looking at me. "They know you like to go out on your own, Wes. They were waiting. Far as we can tell, they sent Lance and his boys there to draw you out."

"Watch now, talk later," Jessica yelled out the window.

"They have our encryption broke too," Sheriff Jackson said. "They knew immediately, we broke their code. They have no clue if we've been recording their transmissions so other than trying to close the trap and find you, they've gone mostly silent."

"How do we know they know we broke their code?" I yelled.

Rolston looked at me, his face stony. "A situation has developed since you've been gone today."

"What?" I asked them.

"Keep your eyes peeled, you never know when they

might be headed this way," Rolston was scanning the sides of the road.

They were doing it again. If I was the so-called figurehead, the guy people looked up to, so why were they treating me like a mushroom? This shit had to stop. I either had to be the man they wanted me to be, or they needed to quit playing coy.

10

THE HOMESTEAD WAS IN AN UPROAR. Angry voices were shouting. Grandma was standing on the porch, leaning against the railing. Raider, for once, was tied off, his leash looped through the log pole that held up the front porch. I bared my teeth in anger. Things must be bad if Grandma had had to restrain my dog. He'd busted out of the house, I was sure, if she'd had to resort to this. My dog looked livid. My mind had considered the possibilities in the bumpy ride back in the back of the truck. Only one thing stood out to me: somebody from our side had alerted the KGR, just like somebody had alerted Spider's crew when we'd grouped up with the state police to free up the slaves that had been captured.

A group of people surrounded a figure on the ground. They were shoulder to shoulder in a semi-circle. Some looked up as we got out of the truck but turned back to the figure. I left my pack in the truck but slung my carbine over my shoulder so I could keep my hands free. Everyone was shouting, cursing. I could hear Raider's response to things; Yaeger and Diesel were barking back in the barn by the sound of it. They weren't happy either.

"Let me through," I said as Sheriff Jackson and Rolston followed in my wake.

I'd ignored the ladies on purpose. I appreciated them coming, but the tensions at the homestead seemed to be rising. Part of that was my fault, and right now it seemed we'd found a traitor in our midst.

"Who is it?" I asked, knowing Sheriff Jackson was right behind me.

"Elias," he said loudly as I wove my way through people.

"Hey—" somebody objected as I tried to push through the inner circle. He saw who it was and put his hands up and slid to the right, jostling people.

The three of us made it inside the inner circle, and a moment later Jess and Emily joined us. Linda was nowhere in sight, but I knew she was either at the radio or somewhere coordinating with our defenses. Elias was bloody from a cut on his temple, and there were scratches and purple marks where he'd gotten bruised. He was rolling on the ground in a near fetal position, his hands and legs cable tied together.

"He wasn't this bad when we left," Jackson said.

Why didn't he do something? Then I realized why.

"I need everyone to get back to what they were doing. This would be a bad time for the Keggers to attack us with everyone all bunched up here, right?" My words thundered above the din of the crowd.

People quieted but didn't start moving out immediately.

"Break it up people," I shouted.

"It's his fault," somebody yelled.

Shouts of agreement came from the crowd. I unholstered my .45 and slowly unscrewed the suppressor, putting it in my back left pocket. The inner crowd had gone silent. I raised it to air and fired a round, making those who hadn't seen what I had been doing flinch.

"Now that I have your attention, I need everyone to get back to what you were doing. Sheriff Jackson, Deputy Rolston and I have this under control. Now MOVE!"

If they didn't listen, things were going to get ugly, but by twos and threes they moved. I put my gun on safe again and holstered it.

"Just a boys' club is it?" Jessica asked from behind me, walking to Elias and hauling him to his feet.

"Sorry, I didn't have time to name off everyone."

"Who did this?" Jackson asked Elias.

"There were so many, I don't know. Somebody pushed me down and then..." he blinked several times, "I didn't want to—"

"Shut up," I told him softly, as his words had made more than a few people pause what they were doing, so I turned to them. "If you folks have nothing to do, the garden could always use weeding."

They hurried out of there, nobody loved weeding. I didn't blame them.

"Should I—" I cut off Emily's words harshly.

"Don't do anything, and keep that big fucking revolver holstered. Elias is going to have a talk with us. You hear me?"

"Wes, I—"

"Not now Emily," I growled.

She looked down, then headed into the house. Grandma had probably stashed Mary inside, reading my old books to keep her out of the chaos. Good. I didn't want Emily to go off half-cocked and kill this man. We had a lot of ground to cover, I needed to be caught up, and this man needed to speak to us.

"That was harsh," Jessica said.

"I don't have time to play games," I spat back, looking at the beaten and bloody state police officer. "Cut his feet loose. We're going to the porch to have a talk."

"So *now* you're in charge?" Jessica asked.

"Jessica, if you're going to keep playing games, please go tag your mom in, and trade spaces with her. Otherwise, please either fill me in or be quiet."

I knew I might have just made a fatal mistake in our relationship, but my blood was up. Not more than a few miles away slaves were working in a farm field, and everything we'd said or done since the failed raid had probably been reported by this man here. Not to mention all the lives lost in the failed raid and the attacks here at the homestead. Was he a plant? Nobody was moving to cut the ties on his feet, so I pulled my own knife and walked up to him.

"If you knee me, kick me or do anything other than hold still, you're going to be sorry." I showed him my knife.

He nodded, and I cut the ties and backed up. He moved his legs, probably to get feeling going again. They had been on there pretty hard.

"My hands?" He held up both hands in front of him, the cuffs biting deep into the flesh.

"Got your cuffs?" I asked the guys with me.

"I've got a set," Rolston said, reaching for a pouch on the back of his belt.

"I want to have a talk, get filled in. Then we can all decide what's going on and what to do about this shit show."

I could hear the usual sounds of the homestead, but with more than the normal raised voices and angry tones. Sheriff Jackson covered him while Rolston cut the ties holding his wrists together and put the cuffs on. Elias thanked him softly and I nodded to the porch. We all walked up that way. Raider had calmed down with the big crowd gone but started growling as soon as Elias got near. Somehow, he knew, my buddy knew.

"Easy big guy. We're going to have a talk. I don't need you to tear his throat out, yet."

"Want me to get my two?" Jess asked.

I looked at her sharply, then nodded. "Jess, I'm sorry, I didn't mean to be so short."

"I know, everyone's blood is up."

"I think we're going to need your mom though. Can you get somebody else to spell her a bit? Maybe have her bring those drugs we got off the clowns?"

Jess nodded and headed to the barn. She was still pissed, but so was I.

"Want me to put your noble beast inside?" Grandma asked.

"Not unless you think Emily and Mary need him," I told her. "He should be good if I take him off his lead now."

"His funeral," Grandma said, shrugging and pointing to Elias.

"It very well might be," I told her.

"We don't just execute people around here," Sheriff Jackson said.

"Actually, if you remember, we've done that a time or two already," I told him.

"That was during an attack, we—"

"Shot a bad guy in the face with a huge revolver that shoots rifle rounds," I reminded him, "after we'd sweated him for information. Don't go soft on me because a traitor is a fellow cop."

"Wes..." Rolston said in a warning tone.

"Listen guys, things around here aren't exactly normal. If I have to skin this man alive for information before slitting his throat or stomping his genitals into a paste to get what I need, I'll do it." This was said for Elias's benefit and I hoped both Rolston and Jackson understood I was playing bad cop, amateur level for sure, but bad cop.

94

"Wes..." Grandma started to say something, while unhooking Raider, "This isn't like you."

"Brave new world," I said through gritted teeth.

Damn, everyone was taking me seriously. Sure, I was mad, and I was sure my tone came out making me sound like a raving lunatic. Linda would have picked up on this, but nobody else seemed to.

"Raider, here," I patted my leg.

He was already moving and bumped me with his shoulder before turning, putting his head under my left hand. I holstered my pistol and pointed at the stairs going up the porch. "Sit," I told Elias.

If my bad cop routine had worked, it didn't show. He sat down, his hands low to cover his midsection like he was going to be hit or kicked again.

"Somebody fill me in please?" I asked.

"Michael was sitting near Linda. I think he's sweet on her, but it took him not two minutes and suddenly he's screaming for somebody to get him a pencil and paper. Linda gave him some and he started writing. He broke the code that fast. We were trying to reach you, but you were on a different frequency. Elias overheard us and slipped out. I thought it was weird, because he was supposed to be changing out one of the guys up the road on lookout. I caught up with him behind the privy, heard him and Spider talking. Fool didn't have his earwig in for some reason. Had him a different radio too, a smaller one, but boy is it slick."

He held up a radio, showing me. It definitely wasn't

anything like I'd ever seen from our guys, nor the captured radios.

"Is this true? You've been working for the KGR?" I asked Elias.

"It's true," Elias said simply, no argument, no begging.

"Why? Have you been working with them all along? Were you a plant from the beginning?"

"Killion has my wife and daughter," Elias said. "Snatched them weeks before we moved on them. Told me unless I want them to come back in pieces, I'd be his inside guy. I ... I talk to them every week. It's the only way I know he hasn't hurt or killed them."

"You betrayed us on the raid where your wife was being held?" Sheriff Jackson asked.

"Yes," he said, tears in his eyes. "I didn't know there was a revolt happening on the back end, and they didn't manage to get out anyway. Killion's got someone else who'd already tipped him off that we were coming, so when he asked me, I had to tell him. He would have killed my family."

"Do you know who that person is?" I asked him.

"No," Elias said, "I wish I did; I would have killed him myself. If we would have broken through his defenses and freed everyone... I wouldn't have had to keep reporting to him. We weren't all organized until the two weeks before the raid. We had been working independently and I'd gone out looking for food ... my family was gone when I got back. Just gone. Then I found the note and the radio..."

"Who roughed you up?" Rolston asked.

"It doesn't matter," Elias told us, "I deserved it."

"I'll be right back fellas," Grandma said and went inside.

Raider turned and barked, and I turned when a return bark came from behind me. Jessica, Linda and her two dogs had come. Linda had the medical bag with the syringes in one hand, a pistol in her other.

"I'm not sure if we're going to need those after all," I said, "sorry. Thought you should sit in on this, though. Elias is going to be telling us all he knows about Spider Killion and his little operation."

"Why did he do it?" Jessica asked.

"Blackmailed. They have his family," I replied.

"You believe him?" Linda asked.

"You're better at this stuff than I am. I don't think we're going to need it to get bloody—"

"I don't know much about his operation, but what I know I'll share. Just please... I don't care what happens to me, but my wife and daughter ... we have to save them."

"It also appears that there's either another plant, or somebody who was monitoring the State Police before the raid who tipped off Killion, if he's to be believed," Rolston said quietly.

The door opened and Grandma and Mary came out. Mary was holding several empty glasses in her hands, and Grandma had a familiar looking pitcher, along with a very familiar looking thermos. She hesitated going near Elias, and then stepped off the porch, handing me the thermos.

"Bottoms up, anyone?" I asked, taking a glass from Mary.

"You're drinking right now?" Rolston asked.

"I'm a moonshiner, not a drunk. I'm pissed but not in a homicidal rage. I'd like a drink to calm my nerves. Would you like a drink? Or just regular lemonade?"

Rolston shook his head, but he was grinning. Jackson was too. They'd finally figured it out; I was playing a role here. Bad cop, good cop, switching things up, baby!

"Can I have something?" Elias asked.

"Regular or unleaded?" Grandma asked him.

"Um... The one with alcohol," Elias said looking at me.

I nodded and poured him a drink from the glass I was holding. The handcuffs made him hold it with both hands, and he thanked me quietly and took a sip. Mary handed me another glass from across the railing. I set it up on the rail and poured myself a drink, then traded the glass's place with the thermos and took a sip. The moonshine and lemonade mixture were perfect. It would have been even better with ice, but we didn't have any at the moment.

After a bit, everyone took a cup and chose their poison. Linda took the thermos and poured herself a cup and dropped me a wink and then nodded at Elias, handing me the thermos. I topped his drink off and he thanked me again.

"We should pull up chairs, this might take a while," Linda said.

"It shouldn't," Elias said. "This has been eating me alive. If I would have held onto the info that you folks had cracked his code, he would have killed my family. By helping you and giving you guys all the information I have ... it's my best chance of keeping them alive long enough for you guys to rescue them.

"You mean 'we' rescue them," I added.

"If I'm allowed..."

"That we will see," Linda said softly.

"Mister Wes, will you read me a story?" Mary asked from my seat on the far side of the porch where she'd retreated to.

"Not right now," I called back softly, "but in a little bit maybe? How about you go check on your mother?"

"She doesn't want me inside right now," Mary said.

Jess and I looked at each other and I put my glass on the railing and jumped the steps past Elias. Jess was fast on my heels. Grandma had barely gotten out of the way when we practically fell through the door. I still had my boots on, and Grandma would whack me upside the head for tracking dirt through her house, but I ran for the back bedroom. Jess smacked into me when I stopped suddenly, my hand trying to turn the doorknob. It was locked.

"What's she—"

I used my shoulder and hip and the door frame splintered, spilling me inside. I let out a deep breath, expecting the worst. What I saw... I was not expecting.

"What are you guys doing?" Emily asked, sitting up from the bed, her face tear-streaked, her cheeks red.

"Mary said you wanted her out of the house, I thought... I don't..."

"We were concerned—" Jessica's words froze as Emily held the BFR up.

"It's unloaded," Emily said. "Here, if you don't believe me," she tossed it on the bed next to her and raised her hands, then stood, spinning in place.

At some point she'd shed the shirt she was wearing and was in a sports bra. The lines of cigarette scars were stark white buttons on her flesh, but as she spun, I saw she was just in her jeans. A fresh shirt laid next to her on the bed, and her old one was wadded up.

"What are you doing?" I asked her, confused.

"I'm ... upset," she said, picking up the shirt she'd been wearing and blew her nose into it, "and embarrassed. You really think I'm crazy?"

"I didn't say that," I said holding my hands up.

"It sounded like you kind of implied that, and you weren't too happy the last time I used that cannon up on the roadway."

"None of us were happy," Jessica said, "with anything, not just you. You just have this habit of using that big honker when we least expect it and at least one time I wasn't done talking to somebody."

"I don't want you guys to think I'm crazy, and no I didn't come in here to kill myself."

I had picked up the BFR and was spinning the cylinder to check if it was loaded, and it wasn't. It was a heavy gun, but finely made, lots of steel. Everything on it was cherry. I was a little envious but knew how much Emily had come to love the thing. A big gun, shot by a petite woman. It was almost a running joke, but nobody did to her face. I knew she was a little unhinged, I knew Jess thought so as well.

"Can I get my shirt on, or are you just going to stare at me?" Emily asked me.

I hadn't been staring at her, I'd been thinking, staring at the BFR I'd put down on the bed next to her.

"I'm sorry, I wasn't..."

Emily cracked a smile and Jessica let out a small laugh, putting a hand on my shoulder.

"I didn't want to go in the other room for tissue," Emily explained, pointing to her old shirt, "I was crying so hard that I had to blow my nose or puke. Sorry shirt, you lost. At least it wasn't one of Wes's socks."

I shook my head and turned around to give her some privacy.

"I'm sorry Emily," Jess started, "I thought the same thing. You've been through a lot and I probably have been treating you like you're a little unhinged."

I winced. I looked over my shoulder to see Emily pull the red t-shirt of hers over her head and smooth the bottom out. I turned back around.

"Maybe I am, but to say what you did in front of a group of people like that?" Her eyes were locked on mine. "It just embarrassed me more than anything else."

"Most of them have seen you shoot at least one guy in the face," I told her softly.

"I'm doing what I think is right," she said, a bit of defiance in her voice, "and when somebody tries to hurt those I care about, they better watch out. I might not be the biggest and strongest momma bear out there, but I sure can bet I'm the meanest." The last was said as she patted the revolver.

"You scare me sometimes," I said suddenly, mentally kicking myself for the words.

"Good, then you're learning," Emily shot back, a smile breaking through.

"I'm never going to understand women," I groaned.

"Maybe we should clue you in?" Jessica asked.

"I would like that, but all of a sudden I'm feeling like I have whiplash," I admitted.

"Why?" Jessica asked.

"Because... What you said the other night."

"What'd she say?" Emily asked.

"Oh, go ahead and tell her," Jessica said with a grin, "it wasn't horrible."

What is going on here?

"She said I always take your side, then walked off in a huff and I didn't see her again until you two were picking me up in the truck. I pissed her off, but I don't know what I did."

"Oh that? Pregnancy hormones are kicking in," Emily said sagely.

"What?" I asked. "Pregnancy hormones?"

"You know how the question goes... What would

you do for a Klondike Bar?" Jessica asked in my ear quietly.

"Yeah?" I said feeling all kinds of confused.

"Plays havoc with your emotions. Makes you hunger for weird things. Peanut butter and pickles, with some chicken in a basket cracker..." Jessica said, a shiver going through her body.

"Oh!!! You should totally try mayo and peanut butter on rye bread!" Emily said pointing.

"I think I'm even more confused than I was before," I admitted.

"Why?" Jessica asked.

"Have you two gotten into Grandma's garden?" I asked them, "Maybe made some home rolls or something? Sounds like a serious case of the munchies to me."

"Pregnancy hormones," they both chorused, then started laughing at the self-jinx.

11

I HATED SPEAKING in front of the crowd that gathered in front of the porch steps. I sat next to Elias who was in handcuffs still.

"So, what he did was due to his family being kidnapped and used as leverage," I finished.

The meeting went late into the night. More than a few people were upset, with calls to lynch him on the spot. Elias got a chance to speak and when he was done, there were more than a few wet eyes, just as many as there were people red in the face from anger. The cook fire was going, and the endless soup or stew was going again, tended by the older daughter of one of the police officers who was staring boreholes into Elias.

Linda had broached with me the idea of keeping Elias in contact with Killion's KGR for misinformation purposes, but neither of us knew who had tipped off Spider. Would they report this back in, if they were even a part of our group? That last bit had been left out on the public briefing we'd held. Tensions were already high, and an air of paranoia had gripped the homestead. I didn't know how to stop it, to fix it. As things broke up, Sheriff Jackson and Rolston stayed behind with Jessica, Grandma, Linda and me.

We were on our third thermos of Grandma's lemonade and instead of making us mellow, the alcohol had made us melancholy. For his protection and ours, Elias had been taken back to the tents, to bunk down with some of the cops back there. He was a broken man, incomplete without his other half and daughter. He was shamed, guilt-ridden and didn't know how to make things better. We had to assume from this point on that Spider had eyes everywhere.

"You know, what did those two fellows have to say that didn't eat a bullet the other night?" I asked Jessica.

"Not much, just that they were supposed to come in, fire on us, attack us, then leave. A quick smash and grab. Obviously, that wasn't all it was, but they were conscripts and weren't part of the larger plan, they hadn't been read in."

"Cannon fodder," I muttered.

"What do you know about that?" Linda asked me.

"I don't know, read it in some of the post-apocalyptic books somewhere. Send the least experienced in first. If they live, they live, if they don't, no big loss. They're used to draw out the targets, so the real hunters can down their game."

"That's pretty much it," Jessica said.

"It's barbaric," Grandma said quietly. "Where's Emily?"

"She fell asleep on the couch with Mary reading to her," I told her. "Raider is keeping watch."

Diesel was sitting at my feet, and I was using him as a surrogate dog, petting him and playing gently with the big beast. Yaeger was happy being wherever Jessica was and was all but laying across her lap, his head touching my leg.

"They're using slaves to work the farms," Rolston said softly, "and in a way, it needs to be done. A lot of things were planted and grew over the summer. Corn and soybeans should be ready soon. Heck, some things are probably already harvested. We should have thought about that when we kept taking in people."

"The land wasn't ours, and it puts too many people away from where we can protect them," Linda shot back.

"I know, I'm just ... what they are doing is terrible, horrible even, but I can appreciate what they're trying to do from a mere theoretical standpoint."

"We need to stop them," Sheriff Jackson said. "Lester says we've got enough equipment right now to arm just about everyone who can fire a gun. But I'm not sure 'everyone' is even enough."

"They have the numbers, the conscripts," Linda said. "Even stashes of food outside their base of operations."

"What?" Jessica asked.

"Remember that stash of food that Emily found?" I

asked her, when she nodded, I went on, "The man I spine shot had been a part of the teams that had stashed stuff. He kept notes in his journal in case he ever needed the info for himself. But there's more stashes than he noted. We know of a dozen locations. Whether or not the food and supplies are there still, I don't know."

"I'm surprised that trailer of food wasn't booby-trapped if it was Spider's," Jessica said.

"According to his notes," Linda answered, "a lot of them are, but the guy Emily killed kept notes of how and where, in case he could find his daughter some day."

"She lives out here?" I asked Linda.

"You didn't read the whole thing?" Linda asked me.

"Pregnancy hormones," I pointed at my temple.

The guys looked at each other in confusion, but the ladies cracked up.

"So, what do we do?" I asked them.

"We go and steal all the supplies we can, and we get our own trap for Spider and his men," Jessica answered immediately.

"How do we do that?"

"I think we have to lure him out. I say we get you on the radio with him and see where things go?"

"I don't think he'd ... wait, would he talk to me you think?"

"He certainly has a hard-on for you," Rolston said, snickering obscenely.

"Ladies present," Grandma scolded.

"Sorry ma'am, but ever since Wes here blew up his camp at the Crater of Diamonds—"

"Lance's camp, but he's not really in charge anymore, is he?" I interrupted.

"I told you it was about revenge," Linda piped back up.

"I know," I said with a sigh; she was right.

"No time like the present, I guess," I said, standing up.

"It's the middle of the night!" Jessica complained.

"Probably when he's moving around in the open, coordinating raids on smaller groups," I shot back.

Jessica put a finger to her lips, tapping them as she thought. Her scars were bright against her tanned skin, though she no longer had any pain from talking. She looked back at me and nodded.

"Goody," Sheriff Jackson said, "now we can play games back." He rubbed his hands together. "Wes, I got to know though, about earlier?"

"I was playing bad cop," I told him, "I thought you guys would have caught on sooner. Sorry."

"A non-cop playing bad cop?" Rolston asked. "I thought *we* were being bad cops and you were a lunatic, raving mad and shouting at everybody."

"I should have seen it sooner myself," Jessica said softly. "He never yells at people."

I bit my tongue and let the lie of omission pass unchecked.

"He's pretty good at it," Linda said. "He had that fella up the hill pissing himself that the dogs were going to eat him. Apparently, the other side has heard stories of what Yaeger, and Raider have done, though I'm not sure they realize that there's two shepherds. Diesel on the other hand..."

The big dog lifted his head up, and I proceeded to scratch behind his ears.

"Just plain looks like a mutant zombie hybrid from the video games. He's a big lover and I doubt he'd really eat somebody."

"I thought he was going to nibble the scalp flaps off that guy's face," I told Linda.

Jessica made an urking sound, putting a hand over her mouth and tried to get up. Yaeger jumped back in alarm and Jessica bolted into the house.

"Ooops," I said, wincing.

Some of the windows were open and we could hear her throwing up, hopefully in the bathroom.

"Might be a good time for you to go make that radio call," Sheriff Jackson told me.

"SPIDER, THIS IS WESTLEY FLAGG, DO YOU READ ME? Over?"

Nothing.

"Spider Killion, this is Westley Flagg. Over?"

A long pause, then a voice broke in.

"Wait one, getting the boss."

"I'm not waiting all night," I told the other side.

We were broadcasting on one of the frequencies

the KGR men had formerly used. I knew now the private frequency Elias had been using, and knew for sure that was being monitored, but I didn't want to endanger Elias's family nor tip our hand in case he didn't know we'd flipped him.

"Mister Flagg," a familiar voice broke into the silence. "Are you ready to meet my terms? Over."

"Spider? That you? Over." I asked, to be sure.

"The same guy you took a shot at back at the Crater of Diamonds, in the flesh. Over."

It was him.

"What are your terms?" I asked, "other than you want ... you know, should we go to a more private frequency, so your entire crew doesn't hear all of this? Over."

"You know, that thought had occurred to me. Your people have proven resourceful in breaking our codes and using encryption. Some here think you're as good as us at it. How about we let our experts on both sides set something secure up and I'll call you back with a frequency and details in twenty minutes? Over."

"Copy that. Twenty Minutes. Out."

"Out."

"Do you think it's a trap?" Rolston asked. As I pulled off the headset and handed it to Michael, the man who'd been getting close to Linda and who had broken the other side's code the last time.

Michael put the headset on and started talking. "Let us know when you're ready," I told him, and he nodded and waved me off.

"Bet on it," I told him, "his traps have traps. In a way, I think we're going to have a hard time trying to outthink a man who's been trying to play chess ten steps ahead of us and cheating at it. I don't know if we can compete directly with that."

"What if *we* cheat?" Sheriff Jackson asked.

"How would we do that?" I asked.

"Get a plant of our own inside there," Linda said immediately, "but it has to be one of the men."

"What?" I asked her.

"You know what they do to the women and children, and there's no guarantee that they won't be traded to another warlord, or whatever Spider calls himself. So, we'd ideally want to put a plant in to join the KGR itself as a first option, or as somebody to work the fields as a worst option," Linda explained.

"So, it'd have to be somebody smart who could think on their feet and make it believable enough that they left our group if asked or confronted. I mean, we're not all unknowns here."

"You guys aren't going to like this," Rolston said, "but I think I should do it."

"What?" we all chorused, loud enough that we were shushed by those in the bunks on the other side of the barn.

"Hear me out. Spider is plugged in with FEMA and DHS, though I doubt they knew what he was doing, and planning to do, or were involved with his debauchery. They probably know I went with the national guard house to house for the manual evacuations. And if their intel is good, and I think it is, they'll know that I asked Jessica out a time or three."

"You did?" Linda asked.

"I knew you were up in the barn; it was the only place that made sense," Rolston said to me. "And no, we never shared a bottle of wine together," he grinned, poking me in the chest, "but I wanted to. Was shot down. Didn't know why, but now I do. I can tell Spider that you ran me out because I made a pass at your girl."

"You have the hots for my girlfriend?" I asked him, chuckling.

"Wait, you didn't ask her yet?" Rolston shot back.

Sheriff Jackson smacked himself across the face lightly and walked back towards the radio.

"Asked me what?" Jessica asked.

"Yes Wes, asked her what?" Linda cooed.

"It's for me to know, and you to find out," I answered, watching her eyes go wide at having her own words used against her.

"You're so sleeping on the couch tonight," she pointed at me.

"Emily is conked out on the couch," I told her.

She turned a furious shade of red in the lantern light. "You know what I mean. The doghouse. The barn!"

"Hey, I was only joking," I told her, "you know that right?"

"You done stepped into it now, son," Linda said, grinning, then turned to walk back to the radio as well.

"You're going to tell me," Jessica said pointing at Rolston, "under threats of pain and death."

"Ma'am, it's Man Law. A guy is already under threat of pain and death for breaking Man Law."

I was nodding my head up and down. "Dude," I said, holding out my knuckles. He didn't leave me hanging and turned himself to go.

"What's this Man Law?" Jessica asked me.

"If we have a son, I'll explain it someday," I told her with a grin.

"You're so infuriating!" She stamped her foot on the ground.

"Shoe, other foot, pot, kettle. You get the idea," I said, chuckling, and went back to the radio, leaving her fuming behind me.

"We set?" I asked, noting Linda had her hands-on Michael's shoulders, massaging them lightly.

"Yeah, just waiting for you. Spider is already back and waiting."

"Ok good. You can stick around; I might need you. Can the rest of you make sure nobody else gets too close?" I asked my core group of friends and soon to be family.

"Sure, expecting to divulge secrets?" Linda asked with a grin.

"Well, Marshall here would be a big one we could use to trip up Spider. We haven't so far, so he knows we know, and we can play that card if we need to. I'm guessing he's using Lance and his gang for local information and muscle. He'll know who the farmers are, who has shady dealings and, if he was into cooking meth like I've heard rumors of, he'd know who to recruit with a cheap high."

Linda was nodding at all of that. "Spider is probably wondering why you didn't do that, to hurt him and their camp already."

"So am I," I said, "but none of us thought of it either, until now."

"We have to get smarter," Jessica said. "It's like we're kids trying to clear the table, while an adult sits back and laughs at us."

"A pool metaphor?" I asked her. "You play?"

"Not much else to do while waiting to go on duty," she said bumping my hip. "But you'll never know. Because you're in the doghouse."

"When isn't he?" Sheriff Jackson asked.

"You're not helping," I muttered, though there were some chuckles as I said it.

"Spider, this is Wes, over."

"Wes, it's just me and my advisors here. I'm sure you have yours around you as well, so let's cut to the chase and get rid of radio formalities."

"Sounds good," I told him. "I suck at remembering what I'm supposed to say at the end half the time anyway."

"As do I, kid. As do I. Are you ready to hear my terms?"

"I don't even know what your terms are, other than you want me and Marshall handed over, or sudden doom, blah blah blah."

"I think we both have underestimated each other a bit here," Spider said coolly. "But in essence, you're right."

"I sort of get why you want Marshall: to keep Lance and his crew of locals working under your thumb. But what I don't understand is, why do you want me?"

"A few things really," Spider said. "At first, my motivations were purely revenge. You almost took me and my top men out with those explosions back at our first base camp at the Crater of Diamonds. We were just getting organized and I had no clue who you were at that point, other than somebody who Lance hated. A squabble over a girl?"

"Yeah, she dumped him for me," I told him.

"I dumped him because he cheated on me," Jess said from behind me, "but I was going to dump him anyways so you could ask me out."

"See?!" Sheriff Jackson interjected, but I shushed him as Spider transmitted again.

He was chuckling. "You see Wes, that's what a lot of men fight over. Women, basically, were created to be companions to the men. Tools to be used to help us prepare our food, rear our children. To be subservient to the men in their lives. God has made them for this purpose only."

The ladies behind me were making puking sounds as his words came out of the small speaker.

"But men fighting over them, well that's natural. It's a battle for the best mates to bed, to raise your children, to build your harem, and raise your own small army of kids. It's a battle so primal that all wars are based on this concept."

"How do you mean?" I asked him, confused.

"It's about power. Pure and simple. Power. Women are a metaphor for things all men fight over. Resources, position in life, respect among others, even marrying off our kids for political or treaty purposes. I know it's convoluted, but I thought it was interesting that, of all things you and Lance had to argue over, it was a woman."

"I won, he lost. What more is there to say?"

"You called me, son; you want something. What is it?"

I thought about that. "For you to stick a shotgun barrel in your mouth and pull the trigger with your big toe."

He chuckled at that, and I heard Jackson snicker. "Doubtful. You know, after I found out that Henry's group were the ones hiding and protecting you, I ordered him to either hand you over, or throw you out for my teams to pick you back up. It was a surprise that he hadn't manipulated or killed off those in his group who didn't have our vision in mind. He was nearing that point when we moved in to get you. Imagine my surprise when I found out he'd had the Marshall bastard too. All of you slipped through his inept fingers and made it back to that quaint little farm shack."

"The quaint little farm shack that's repeatedly kicked your ass every time you've sent men against us, not to mention us taking out your APC."

"Yes, I hadn't thought your people to be clever enough. I was originally sending enough people to not only wipe out all the men, but to bring back the women and children here to me. That same day I underestimated your group as badly as you underestimated mine."

117

"Why are you taking the women and children?" I had to know.

"Haven't you been listening boy? It's power, plain and simple. You hold a gun on man's wife, threaten to rape his sixteen-year-old daughter repeatedly in front of her, and send the tape to him after you kill them both, you can twist him into doing anything, anything at all. Power."

I was thinking of Elias, and I was sure I wasn't the only one. Had he slipped up here, or was he sending me a subtle message that he knew we'd flipped him?

"Yet you still would leave us alone if Marshall and I turn ourselves in. Why?"

"I found out more about you. Oh, I know you won't come to me willingly, but I had my men go upstate and pull your college records after that bloody nose you gave me. Seems you're a gifted chemist and, from what Lance tells me, a rather good moonshiner. I'd have you for those skills, if nothing else, but you're a thinker. With some time and persuasion, I think you'll see that what I'm doing is necessary if this society is to pull itself up by the bootstraps from the collapse."

It was what I thought. I could hear the noises of people behind me in the barn, sleeping, talking quietly. Those standing around me were silent though, all looking at me expectantly.

"And, you want me to cook drugs for you?" I asked him.

"Among other things," Spider said. "If society is to be reborn, it's easier to have subservient serfs to do the work. If a few die from overdoses, well, that's a couple of less mouths to feed. It's not like the government has done much better, by the way. Did you know most of the population centers that FEMA sent the citizens to are overridden with diseases, drugs, crime and violence? Worse than out here, by an order of magnitude."

"So, you're suggesting an un-civil society in order to rebuild society as we knew it?" I asked him.

"Among other things," he said, with amusement in his voice. "I must say, it really is delightful to talk to a learned man such as yourself. I could really find myself liking you, until I remember you almost killed me by surprise."

I grinned at that last bit; I should have shot him. I'd almost died by sticking around too long, but that was beside the point.

"I'd never go willingly with you Spider," I told him. "Why not turn loose your slaves, quit the abuse and try working as a benevolent leader instead of a ruthless overlord?"

"I had considered that," Spider said in an oily voice, "but there's no real fun in it. Besides, I've been in conflicts all over the world. I've seen governments collapse and anarchy reign. I've been in Africa and the Middle East, watching first one dictator after another be replaced. I learned history from watching them, I know what they did wrong. When you're as close to the problem as they were, they never saw the coup coming that took them out of the equation. Long have I foreseen the fall of the United States, and I prepared, much like you probably have. Much like Henry's survivalist group did as well. But to turn away useful serfs when so much is needed to be done this first year? No, I cannot and will not."

"So, you're setting yourself up as King of this area?" I asked in disbelief.

"Do you read the bible?" he asked simply.

"Not always. Running moonshine was always a Sunday thing, kept the busybodies out of windows. Hard to get too religious when I never went to church."

"I would encourage you to read Psalm 145," Spider said, "because someday, that's how the people of this area, and maybe even this state, will see me. Not as the man who temporary enslaved them, made whores of their wives and children. I will be remembered as a great savior who led his flock out of the darkness and into the light."

I was sitting there in shock, not believing what I was hearing.

"You're pretty religious and educated for a dumbass biker," I said into the microphone.

The others around me shifted, Jess giving me a wan smile. Linda looked amused at my quip as well. They knew I was goading him.

"I ride bikes, because I like to feel the power between my knees, wouldn't you? Hmmmm? At least I'm not a hypocrite about what I am, who I am, who I will become."

"How does that make me a hypocrite?" I asked him.

"Because even your own people recognize you're the leader who doesn't want the job, won't do the work. You're selfish, your family lives in the big house while they are in a barn and tents, and you've got a harem of ladies taking turns warming your bed. You're just like me, but you wrap yourself in this faux righteousness that churns my stomach."

I pushed back from the radio a moment, my hands shaking. He couldn't have gotten all of that from Elias, and he was wrong on a lot of points, but he was half right on others. I *felt* that more than I could analyze it. I looked behind me and Jessica stood there, her mouth open in shock. The Sheriff was writing notes furiously in a notebook he'd taken from the table where I'd first sat at with Grandpa's old base station.

"Truth hurts? Doesn't it?" Spider asked.

"You've got it wrong in a way," I told him. "Even if Marshall and I turned ourselves in, would you release your slaves?"

"No." Spider was quick to basically repeat his answer from earlier.

"Yet you expect us to do that, and we're basically at a stalemate. You can't come get us yourself."

"And you can't come free the slaves, nor stop me from gaining power and growing my influence," Spider said before I could form the next thought.

"That's possible," I told him quietly. "What would it take for you to leave our group alone entirely? No more attacks, no more loss of life on either group's side?"

"I want Marshall for sure, but what I want are your

services," Spider said emphatically. "Oh, I'm not talking about taking you, I'm talking more your skillsets. Alcohol, chemicals ... drugs... That'd be a good start, but first I want your women."

"What?" I asked him, outraged.

"Not the whole group's ladies, just your harem of bitches. You've opposed me at every turn and cost me dearly. I want to take something of yours in repayment. I want your harem. I understand the one you're about to marry is pregnant with your bastard, isn't that right?"

Jessica gasped behind me and I took a deep breath, my brain starting to fog with anger for him ruining that.

"No, I'm not giving anyone to you," I said simply.

"Oh, I'm not done yet," Spider said, and I felt somebody's hand start kneading my shoulders. "Next I want her mother. I hear she's quite the looker, a little long in the tooth, but looks like she's mid-thirties. You've gotten a taste of her by now, or so I've been told. You two have gotten extra cozy since she tried to shoot you. Been spending time together alone," I heard Jessica make a rude sound behind me, "and lastly, I want that little crazy blonde bitch that's been executing my men. I hear she's quite the spinner. I'd have her as my own *personal* slave. Send me those three, and then we'll discuss you providing services as my men need it. You never know, you may soon grow to enjoy our mutual association and join me someday. I can always use a man as educated and skilled as you."

"No," I told him. "I was merely curious and wondering if you were a reasonable man. I don't think any of us could come to an agreement under those terms."

"You know, your inner circle, your inner cadre? Be careful of who you trust. Oh, I'm sure you've got plants of your own in my camps already, just as I have many in yours, but the jealousy they feel for what you have, for what you've done, and what you've accomplished, is growing. I fear for your safety. If anybody is to kill you, I'd rather me be the one to pull the trigger, than one of your more trusted advisors. Et tu, Brute?" He laughed.

"Spider..."

"Besides, I've got more personal reasons for wanting you here with me now. I'll take your services to start, but eventually, you'll be mine. Bye." The transmission cut off abruptly.

I tried to reach him more, but he'd gone for the night. With it, so had my sleep, and my paranoia had shot through the roof. I turned to see it was Linda Carpenter who'd been kneading my shoulders. She stepped back, but I noticed the look Jessica was giving her mother before she turned her head. Anger. Hurt. Suspicion. I shuddered, wondering what or who was going to be the one sticking a knife in my back. He really thought I had a harem. I closed my eyes to breathe. My head swam some, my tongue was dry. A drink, I needed a drink.

"Where are you going?" Sheriff Jackson asked as I got up quickly.

"You all heard him," I said, gesturing at the radio. "What do you think?"

"I think he's been telling a lot of lies," Linda said, "I tried to kill you, not sleep with you. Sorry kid, you're not my type."

"And for one of us to be jealous and betray you?" Rolston asked, "I don't see that happening. At all."

"I need a drink," I said, starting to walk. "Jessica, you coming?" I asked holding my hand out.

She shook her head and stepped out of the lantern's soft glow. I heard her footsteps retreating for a few moments and then walked past the rest of the group and to the house. Grandma was on the porch steps. She saw the look on my face and pushed her foot against a clear glass one-gallon carboy. I nodded and picked it up and pulled the stopper. She kicked me in the shin.

"What?" I asked her.

"Use a glass, you savage," she said pointing to the empty tumbler sitting next to my chair. "I knew this might be a mistake, you and that snaky Spider talking."

"Nothing got accomplished, except that Spider had somebody close enough to us to ruin my proposal to Jessica."

"I knew you were gonna pop the question sooner or later, but you never talked to me about it," she said, kicking me in the shin again, despite not losing pace in her rocking.

"I know... Linda pressed me on the issue, and I told her I wanted to, but I was going to find the right time to do it and do everything right. I don't even have a ring to give to her when I ask her, and right now she's so pissed at me..."

Grandma pulled her wedding band off slowly, then held her fist up over my hand, "It was your Grandpa's grandmother's. It was to be passed down," she said pressing it into my hand. "So now I did. So, you going to go pop the question tonight?"

I slid the ring into my pocket and shook my head. The only thing that would fix this funk was more drinking. I poured myself an inch in the glass and took a sip. It had been proofed, but the unaged corn liquor still had a lot of bite to it. I kicked my feet up and looked at the sky. Why was I being tested so? That was all I wanted to know. Why? I took another sip. Grandma got up and patted me on the shoulder, then headed in. I sat outside, drinking to drown my thoughts and thought of God, of the Bible. What I remembered of it. Never more than this moment had I wished I had more faith in ... well, everything, including God and Jesus himself.

Despite being surrounded by an entire army of people, and family, friends and loved ones, I felt alone. So very, completely alone.

13

GRANDMA, Mary or Emily who'd fallen asleep on the couch had let Raider out of my room. The sun was shining bright, and that was what finally woke me. Little jackhammers were at work behind my eyes and I felt like a baby dragon had used my mouth as a potty chair. I tried to get up, but my head seized in what felt like a vice and I laid back down, nauseous.

"Is he awake?" I heard Jess from the hallway.

"No, passed out early this morning. Hasn't come out yet." Emily's voice.

"Can this wait?" Grandma asked.

"No, it can't," Jessica replied, her voice sharp.

"Momma said he's sleeping ugly. I'm pretty sure that means no clothes, but I didn't see him," Mary piped up.

Raider must have been by the door also, because I heard him let out a low woof. I looked down; I was still dressed in yesterday's clothing. I had managed to kick my boots off when I'd stumbled in, but I didn't remember laying down.

"Sorry folks, I want to talk to him alone. If I need to sit and wait for him to come out of his alcoholic stupor, I will."

"Give him these," Grandma's voice.

The door opened, and I winced at the sound of the hinges squeaking and the way the wood at the top of the door rubbed when the air got humid in the fall. She saw my eyes open and she nodded, then closed the door behind her. She walked over and set a small bottle of pills next to the bed. Excedrin migraine with caffeine! And a big glass of water. I wanted to talk, but she sat at the foot of the bed, just far enough away that I could only touch her with my foot. My mouth felt glued shut with crud.

"You heard that?" she asked, nodding to the hallway.

I tried to nod in response, but bolts of agony shot out of my eyeballs and I moaned, putting my hands over my eyes.

"Too hungover to talk?" she asked.

I made a weak thumbs-up sign.

"Well, tough shit, I'll make my questions easy for now, then. Since I'm pregnant I have to know, and I can't live not knowing. I already know most of the answers already, so don't lie. Got it?"

I made a thumbs up sign again after taking my hands off my eyes. She nodded.

"Did you sleep with my mother? Did you have sex with my mother?"

I couldn't shake my head either, so I tried to make a thumbs down sign with my left hand over my chest. She seemed to get it and nodded.

"I know Emily is in love with you," she whispered silently, "and I know you've looked at her, I've seen it myself. Are you sleeping with Emily?"

Thumbs down.

"Did you ever?"

Thumbs down.

She took a deep breath, then stood, pacing the room, one hand on her forehead. After a moment, she turned away from me.

"Were you going to propose to me?" Her back was turned to me, she was scared to know.

She didn't turn right away, but when she did, she saw the ring I was holding in my right hand. I'd snaked it out of my pocket when her back had been turned.

"Are you proposing to me right now?" She asked, a sob escaping her lips.

Thumbs up.

She started crying and then sat next to my chest, slowly pulling my shoulders upright. I fought down the nausea as she kissed my forehead and pulled my pillows behind my back, using her legs to cradle my head. She grabbed the pills and pressed them to my lips. I took them and waited for her to put the glass to my lips. I swallowed them down. Then I reached up for the glass and downed the contents entirely.

"If we're going to have a family together, you can't get that blind stinking drunk, ever again," her words came out over half a sob, half a gasping breath.

I started to give her a thumbs up, but the water had done wonders for my mouth and throat, though I was still nauseous.

"I don't ever want to drink again," I said quietly.

She hugged me close.

14

"I DON'T KNOW who to trust," I told Jessica the morning after an entire day lost to a hangover.

Linda, Jessica, Emily and Mary were sitting at the table, having breakfast with Grandma and me.

"I don't either," Jessica said. "Mom, do you know if any of what Spider said was true? Not about the ... harem stuff, but the other things?"

Grandma shifted in her seat uncomfortably when 'harem' was mentioned. Yesterday she'd thought it was hilarious that people thought I was not only in a relationship with Jessica, but with her mother as well as Emily. I sort of understood the ribbing about Emily, but she'd become such a close friend that denying anything had backfired on me.

"I've got my notes here," she said, having brought them for a brainstorming session.

"What about people being jealous of us living in the house, having and hoarding food? He didn't quite say it like that, but you know what I mean?" I asked, trying to move the discussion along a bit.

"Well..." Linda put her notebook down, "yeah, some of them are a little resentful about that. It's probably where the rumors of your 'harem' started. Jess and Emily had traded your room back and forth for a while, you taking the couch. I know you two didn't want to just ... shack up," she said looking at Jessica, "but it doesn't bother me, and I don't think Mrs. Flagg minds Jess staying with you."

"Wait, really?" I asked her.

"Yeah, not all of these people were prepared. Right now, they're looking at every meal and comparing it to what they used to have. Trust me, food is food when it comes to survival, but not a lot has changed for you and your Grandma."

"Wait, what's a harem?" Mary asked.

"I don't think you should—" Grandma started to say, but Emily cut her off.

"They think Mister Wes has a bunch of girlfriends." She tapped her daughter on her nose.

Mary scrunched up her face at that and took another bite of the plain oatmeal we'd cooked this morning, fortified with honey and some dried fruit. I looked at my own steaming bowl, thinking about Linda's words.

"I don't have enough of my food storage to share with everyone. As it is, I might have a year's worth for just me and Grandma if we're being frugal, and we really haven't been."

"I know, and deep down, they probably know that too. Besides, some of these people here were not quite preppers, but they had a lot more than others. A soccer mom who pops into the deli for dinner instead of cooking a few days a week? A trucker bachelor who only has a few simple meals, because he used to eat out of the wheel of death at truck stops? Those are the ones hurting now."

"Lord, how do you keep the peace in the barn?" I asked her.

Before Linda could answer, Emily patted her holster. "Superior firepower makes a fine negotiating tactic."

"I don't even understand how a bitty thing like you can shoot that," Grandma said.

"Let's go fire it later on today. It's really not that bad. It intimidates the boys. Right Wes?" The last bit was said sweetly, and I almost avoided rolling my eyes.

"It's pretty scary when you're holding it," I admitted.

"See? Works on our fearless leader, it'll work on anybody!"

She was joking, but only Mary was smiling.

"What about the other stuff? Like, how did he know I was about to propose to Jessica?" I asked.

"How many people did you tell?" Linda asked me.

"Before it was outed... I guess it was you and the guys on the hill when we were interrogating that guy at the outpost?"

"So that would be Jackson, Rolston, Curt, and that other dude?"

"Other dude," I said, smiling. "I know the face, he came in with the State Police, but I think he's retired military. Not a cop. Can't think of the name. You remember, Jessica?" I asked her.

"Luke, and he's the guy you found in the woods," Jessica shot back.

I snapped my fingers. "That's it. The one who'd been held hostage."

"That's the one."

"Ok, so that's a small group. I wonder who they told?"

"I think you're forgetting something here," Grandma said. "Wes rather loudly announced that Jessica was having a baby. It would be about any southerner's assumption that they were going to get married."

I grunted; she was right. I took another bite of my oatmeal and washed it down with coffee. Should I feel guilty that I'd scraped together the money to buy all this food? We had enough carrots and potatoes downstairs that we could have lived on that for a time, but not long term, and especially not if we wanted potatoes to replant for next season.

"What do we do about this mess?" Emily asked.

"We have to play the game five steps ahead of the ten steps Spider is already ahead. It sounds to me he used Henry and Lance as local access, but he's really the one in charge. We have to turn the tables on him somehow," Linda said firmly.

"I think we need to find whoever else is informing on us. We've got more people here, Spider admitted as much."

"He said it was somebody in your inner circle. I don't even know who that is exactly," Emily replied.

"Well it's all of us here, especially Miss Mary"—the little girl beamed at being recognized— "then Sheriff Jackson, Deputy Rolston, Curt, Lester... Who else am I missing?"

"That's a big pool of people, and I don't believe none of it," Grandma said. "One of us betraying you? If the sheriff or deputy wanted to cause you trouble, they already would have. Besides, I trust all of you."

"Even me?" Mary asked.

"Even you, sweet pea."

I grinned at that; Grandma used to call me that when I was little. I'd grown out of that nickname quick enough.

"What if we keep doing what we were doing, and see if we can trip the informer up somehow?" I asked, an idea forming.

"What do you have in mind?" Emily asked.

"With the right bait, maybe we can force the hand of both Spider and the informers?" I asked the table aloud.

"Bait? You?"

"Me, and not just me. No way would I risk Marshall, he's too..."

"Innocent," Emily finished.

"Not when you're done with him," Jessica mused.

"My momma and Marshall?" Mary asked, her eyes getting big.

"No, no, no, no," Emily said laughing, "they're just teasing me. Mr. Marshall kind of asked me out on a date some time."

"So, it's like a Tuesday or Wednesday thing? Because those are the only days, he doesn't do the reading; it's when Miss Carla does the math stuff."

I snorted and kept eating.

"You have an idea in mind," Linda said noting my smirk.

"Yeah, let's go do some damage to them. He for sure wants five of us. What if the four of us," I said pointing to Linda, Jessica and Emily, "all go out on a hunting expedition. See if somebody lays a trap like they tried to do at the old farm?"

Linda tapped a finger on her lips, a gesture I noticed both mother and daughter shared when thinking.

"If the traitor or traitors are too squirrely, they won't call out, and we do some harm. Start putting fear into the KGR's people. If they do try to alert them so they set up a trap ... we leave Michael, Jackson and Rolston here and they can get word to us and coordinate things at this end and try to take two birds with one stone?"

"As far as plans go, it sucks," Jessica said, "But I don't see any downside. They'll slip up, especially with

Elias now outed here. Plus, if we can get his family out before Spider finds out he's been flipped...?"

"What if we bring Elias with us? Maybe somebody who's been at the larger camp?" I asked.

"No, if he's recognized, his family is dead. Hm... What about Lucas... Luke?" Jessica asked.

"He would have an inside view of how the camp is run, but would we need him if we're going to do some far sniping? Or do you really want to go in there and start fires and blow things up?" I asked.

"How utterly nefarious of you Westley," Linda said, "I think you're perfect for my daughter. The ring is lovely by the way."

Grandma beamed.

"So, you want to do that?" I asked her.

"Sure, unless you have a better idea." Linda responded.

"I'm in," Emily said at once, "if you'll watch Mary for me, Grandma."

"I'd love to, she's a lovely child," Grandma said, patting Mary's hand.

"Hey Wes, you still have that Saran Wrap?" Jessica asked, an evil grin lighting up her face.

"I wonder if we should start hitting the food stores," Emily said. "Full bellies would stop what sounds like a slowly starting rebellion. That trailer of food we got was nice, but it's going fast."

I thought about that and nodded. If we were careful, we could maybe accomplish a couple of things.

Food, and set traps of our own. I started smiling and nodding.

"You've got an idea," Jessica said, grinning.

———

SOMEBODY HAD SCORED A COUNTY MAP WITHIN AN HOUR of us asking around, and I spent that time with the girls marking out the locations that the man I'd spine shot had put in his journal. There was more than I'd realized, as I'd only skimmed the material before giving it to Linda. We were going to keep this one close to the vest, real close.

"Who do we take?" Jessica asked me.

"If Sheriff Jackson doesn't have any objections, I think it should be you, me, your mom and the IED guy, Paulson. Keep things small. We'll have to have trucks with us, radios. We hit one location, check it for traps, steal the food, set traps of our own, and go onto the next location."

"Four doesn't sound like a lot though," Jessica said softly.

"You don't want me to go?" Emily asked.

"I'd rather... What I'm saying is—"

"You're needed here," Grandma cut in. "Your Mary is a sweet one, but she needs you. She worries, you know? Besides, we're talking about grabbing food, not setting the bigger trap yet."

"She does? But I'm fine, I've always been ok going

with you guys before," she finished, a look of confusion on her face.

"Poor girl has been clinging to me or Wes every time you're not around. Neither of us mind, but she's been having nightmares lately," Grandma told her.

"I didn't realize..." Emily started, letting her words trail off.

"Just this one trip. There's going to be lots of opportunities to get the bad guys," I told her, grinning.

"You're right," Emily said. "I just... When I go with you guys, I feel like I can contribute, instead of being a drag on everyone."

"You're not a drag on us," Linda told her. "You've proven time and time again that we can rely on and trust you. It was you more than anyone else who got Wes back on his feet when we thought we were going to lose him."

"Jessica did a lot of that," Emily shot back, but she wasn't snarking, more like stating fact.

"I did," Jessica said, "but look at it like this: Wes can move silently through the woods and is almost as good or equal shot to my mom. I was military, Mom was ... well, we don't talk about that, but my Mom has got a certain skill set."

Linda looked uncomfortable about that, and a lot of people had been wondering exactly what her experience was. It was a mystery wrapped in an enigma, to borrow a phrase.

"And we could use the IED guy, Jay Paulson, to disarm any bombs we find or set our own."

"Do we still have those triggers grandpa made?" I asked Linda.

"We've got a few left, plus a dozen or so that I had some of our more bored men in the barn make," Linda's eyes twinkled at that. "The question is, can you make more of that generic Tannerite?"

"Yeah, but we'll need something for shrapnel if we really want it to be nasty."

"I got that covered too," Linda said, grinning. "I've been talking with Jay."

I grinned; it was coming together.

15

"Linda said you could use a hand?" Paulson asked the next morning.

Jay Paulson was an interesting guy. I'd been told he'd walked away from a successful career in the corporate world after 9/11. He'd personally lost family in the towers; his brother had been trapped inside during the first collapse. He'd quit his job that day and had enlisted with Uncle Sam's Misguided Children. Crayon eaters is what Linda had said, though a bit affectionately.

"I can, did she read you in on what we're going to do?"

"Steal the bad guys' food, blow up the bad guys?" he asked, a mischievous grin on his face.

"That's the plan. I'm worried about innocents stumbling on things though," I told him, "and setting the traps off."

"If the drops are as hidden as that trailer was, it

won't be likely any innocents will be coming to get them, before Henry or Spider go to fetch them."

"So, you're ok with kind of doing the opposite of what you were trained to do?" I asked him.

"Sure, I mean, I have to know how to make the bombs, and set the traps, if I'm to spot them, disarm them first. Have to hope that Spider doesn't have a guy like me on his staff though."

"I know," I said softly, "you any good?"

He held up his hands in front of me. "Got all my fingers and limbs. What do you think?"

I grinned. "What about what we've got to work with?"

"Crude, but it should get the job done, and sort of impressive you figured out how to cobble it together from everyday type of things."

"I was a chemistry major in college," I admitted.

"You and I are going to have a lot of fun," he said, tipping his boonie hat at me.

I grinned and put my fist out, he bumped it and we walked to the first set of trucks. To begin with, we'd take one, do our thing, set the bombs and bring it back here to be unloaded, switching trucks so we wouldn't lose time. The motors roaring up and down the silent county would probably confuse Spider's lookouts at first and we hoped to hit at least half of the marked stops before he got wise to it. Hopefully we'd have three-quarters of them emptied before he could assemble a team.

"You're packed pretty heavily," he said noting the

M4 I'd started taking with me, along with the pistol, extra mags, the radio and my backpack.

"And you're not?" I asked him noting he had almost the exact same gear as I did.

"You're a civilian," he said, grinning. "No offense intended, it just looks like you know how to use that."

"Sort of," I told him. "Took this off a guy who almost killed me."

"What happened to him?" he asked.

"Wes did," Jessica said hopping in the bed of the truck, her hand going out to Linda who was stepping over the side.

I wasn't driving Linda's truck this time, but like hers, this one had a rear window that opened in the back and was a stick. When a design feature worked, all manufacturers seemed to copy each other.

"You want to ride shotgun, ma'am?" he asked Jessica.

"Not this time," she said, "but I might on the way back."

Jay nodded. "All right."

I fired up the truck and pulled out slowly. Each point on the map had been marked out so I knew how to get there from two or three directions, which meant if a fast exit was needed, I had a lot of options. Our first spot was to the first place we'd found the food. It was the closest spot on the map. The plan had been to park half a mile out, and the ladies would jog in. I had my misgivings about Jessica jogging and crawling through the weeds with her being pregnant, but her and her mother were great scouts. They'd radio us if the coast was clear.

Doing this, we'd be able to clear an area in three hours or less, or until we lost light. I still had my NVGs and they were in the backpack, but we didn't have enough for everyone and having one out of four wasn't odds I liked. Besides, I had plans for those later on down the road.

I made the turn and thought about the missing trailer. We'd just pulled that one out of there, but if we stacked enough debris back up, the KGR's would have to dig through it to see it'd been taken, by which time, it'd be too late.

"So, what were you doing before the collapse?" Jay asked.

"Honestly? I was waiting to start a job as a science teacher. Before that, I ran moonshine with my Grandpa."

Jay threw back his head and laughed. "No shit?"

"No shit," I said with a grin. "I ran a bunch of it not too long ago."

"I'd heard about that, but I wasn't sure it was true."

"How come?" I asked him.

"You know, the stories they tell about you and your ladies?"

"I don't ... and my ladies?" I wasn't being suspicious much, but the potential for learning the gossip was too rich to pass up.

"Your girlfriend, her mom, Emily and her daughter. Sounds like you've been raising hell ever since the collapse happened, doing what you can to fight. Gotta admire that."

"Thanks," I said, relieved I wasn't sitting with somebody who thought I was a harem type of guy.

"And the more outlandish stuff I've heard, I figured it was either tall tales or misinformation."

"What...?"

He laughed. "Oh, there's some folks that think you're hogging all the pretty ladies, but hell, I couldn't keep one lady happy, let alone three. Reason why I've stayed single. I figured those stories were embellished a bit."

"Jessica's the only one I'm involved with," I told him.

"Oh, I know. I told the others I figured Emily was an overprotective sister, the way she's always around you. You're doing a good thing, helping her with Mary."

That wasn't exactly right, but I didn't want to go down that road, so I simply said, "Thanks."

"They also say you're some kind of master hunter, master sniper, master survivalist and arrogant as all get out."

Ouch.

"Sorry if I've given anyone that impression." What else could I say?

"I'll say this, with you as an organizer, you've done a hell of a job. I really appreciate you and Les pulling everyone together. Sleeping in a barn is a hell of a lot better than what I was doing when I was trying to stay away and ahead of the KGR. Plus, I did mention I don't believe half the outlandish stuff. You seem pretty down to earth to me."

"Now you're making me blush," I said teasing him. "Do you like red or blue crayons?"

"You shithead," he said, laughing. "Bribing me with food already?"

"Linda told me the joke," I admitted. "I don't actually know the reference."

"It's like—"

Jessica banged on top of the cab, reminding me we were fast approaching the drop-off point. I pulled off to the side and shut down the truck.

"All right, you boys watch this side, we'll radio when it's clear to come in."

"How about I just head in with one of you and get started on things, while the others come in?" Jay asked.

Actually, that was a good point.

"Mom and I have worked together on stuff like this, it's kinda like..."

"You're battle buddies; you know what your team is going to do without looking or asking?" Jay asked.

"Pretty much, plus, we can cover a lot of ground faster than you boys can," Linda said.

"Hey, I know I've been out of the services a few years, and I'm not out of shape. Much."

Jessica grinned and put her earpiece in. I did likewise, and with that the conversation was over. I made sure I pocketed the keys and the both of us headed for the tall grass next to a house that looked like it hadn't been lived in since the collapse. It was across the road from where I'd pulled the truck over, but it was on slightly higher ground.

"Check the windows?" Jay asked.

"Sure, I got the front?"

"Works for me," he said, moving his way slowly around.

I was careful and didn't just peer into the windows, I crawled up to one of them, though the sound of the truck would have alerted anyone we were there. I didn't want to get a shotgun to the face in case somebody was, so I was careful. Peeking inside though, I could see a heavy layer of dust on the hardwood flooring into a living room. There was a set of prints that were probably left by a small animal. Cat maybe? Not many, just a couple of sets. I moved to the next one and looked. Much of the same.

"Looks abandoned," Jay said into the earpiece.

"Same. Dust everywhere, no human prints. Maybe cat?"

"Have eyes on the cat," Jay said. "It's ... not alive anymore."

I cringed. The ladies would have heard all of that but were moving fast and silent so they wouldn't have answered.

"Looks empty. Want to set up near the front porch, where we have some cover?" I asked.

"Sounds good."

In a couple of moments, he walked in as low as he could go, his rifle out in front of him. I motioned for him, he saw me and joined me near the corner of the cement porch stairs.

"The cat...?" I asked him.

"Looks like it got in somehow and couldn't get back out. Sorry," he said. "One of the other things I've heard about you is that you're a big animal guy, a modern-day Dr. Doolittle."

I shook my head, and he chuckled softly.

"People are going to invent stories, for better or worse."

"Lately," I whispered, "it's been for worse." I didn't quite want him to read him into everything, I really didn't know him that well.

"True that."

We sat and listened. What felt like an hour later, we got our first check in from Linda and Jessica.

"We're in a place to observe the farm," Linda's voice came over the earpiece. "Girl Scout is making a sweep."

"Copy," Paulson said into his radio.

"All clear, come in with the truck. We're moving to a position to cover you should people have moved in behind us, though I doubt it. This is a pretty dead area."

"Ok," I told her. "See you in a few."

WE PULLED THE TRUCK RIGHT UP TO THE BARN. THE ground was dried and cracked, so I didn't have to worry about leaving tracks. I helped the ladies prop up some of the fallen timber and sections of the roof that had been covering up the trailer. The last of it was finished by Jay who'd used the trigger Grandpa had designed, along with a coffee can full of the special sauce. Bits of rock and scrap metal from the junk behind the barn had been added. It wasn't going to be perfect, but whoever pulled the sheet of plywood back to look for the trailer was going to get a very unpleasant surprise.

"Rock and Roll!" Jay said with a grin.

"Time for the real work to begin," Linda said.

I nodded.

"After that jog, I'm riding with you," Jessica said, poking me in the side. "Shotgun!" she announced.

Jay bowed graciously.

16

THE NEXT LOCATION on the map we'd marked was on the northwestern section of the county. It was the furthest out, and one we'd argued that would least likely be watched by Killion's men. It was also the most likely one to have been emptied by them, as it was the furthest away from their base and normal operations. Again, we stopped a good half a mile or more away from the location. When Jess went to get out, Jay gently pushed her door closed.

"Ma'am, I'd appreciate it if you sit this one out. I could use the exercise."

"I ... oh hell," Jess said, then nodded.

Jay and Linda took off at a fast walk, being careful of their movements. This area was wild, dotted with farms and fields that had long gone fallow, with weeds and trees growing up in what, years ago, had been hay, soybean, corn and sometimes sunflowers. Jess and I had pulled off into the edge of one, where the ground was firm. It didn't hide the truck entirely, but it was better than parking it on the side of the road.

"So how was Jay?" Jessica asked as we moved away from the truck in case it was noticed and targeted by sadistic mutant muppets from a Jim Henson nightmare.

"When we were waiting?" I asked her.

"Yeah."

"Well... I found out some interesting things about myself," I told her quietly. "Apparently there's a ton of wild rumors going around."

"Well, I knew that," Jessica said.

I snapped my head in her direction, surprised, noting the grass moving over her shoulder; there was something headed our way. I tried not to grin.

"Why didn't you say anything?" I asked her.

"Girls talk. You boys have Man Law, girls have Girl Talk. Deal with it."

"Seriously?" I asked her.

She grinned and shook her head no. "Just messing with you. I sometimes hear snippets from the children or other ladies, rarely the men. I usually try to put down some of the wilder rumors and explain how things actually happened, but sometimes I let them grow and let people think what they will."

"I can't believe this," I said softly.

"Look!" Jess pointed to her left.

The tall weeds were moving about twenty yards to her left now.

"I've been watching it. I think it's probably a deer or

something. I was about to warn you in case I can bring home some venison tonight on top of things…"

"Does anything get past you?" Jessica whispered.

"Not when it can go in my belly." The last bit was done in Fat Bastard's voice from Austin Powers fame… Then I fell silent as a head popped up.

It was a buck, and I could tell it was a big one. He'd heard us and snorted, stamping the ground. I couldn't see that, but I could damn well hear it. I pulled my M4 up to my shoulder and flicked the safety off just as its head went down. Jess scooted backward without asking. She was out of the muzzle flash range, but with the suppressor on, it had still been within a couple feet in front of her face. The deer heard that too, and took off bounding, first to the left, then straight away from us.

I stood in one smooth motion, once again sighting it in the scope, and slowly timed the bounds, before squeezing the trigger. The gun made a clacking sound as the bolt worked, the empty shell casing ejected, and a fresh one was locked and ready. The grass was thrashing, and the buck wasn't bounding any more. I'd hit him, but how well?

"And his legend grows! AHHHHHHHH!" Jess said, standing, shaking her hands in the air of mock applause.

"You obviously want to gut this one, don't you?"

Jessica shook her head quickly, one hand going over her mouth.

"That's what I thought," I told her, grinning. "Cover me," I said, putting my gun on safe.

Jessica followed, but kept her distance so she could keep an eye on both me and the truck. I found the deer still thrashing. My shot had taken it just above the shoulders near the spine. It wasn't quite done yet, so I finished it off with my knife and waited. I was glad Jess hadn't watched that part. I waited, crouched down. If she hadn't been pregnant would this have grossed her out so much? I always considered myself a simple guy. I loved to hunt, fish, look for diamonds, run some liquor through the stills ... but girls, marriage, pregnancy? That hadn't been on any immediate plans, until they were. I hadn't spent the time or energy to think about it much. But it now occupied my mind in a running loop in the back of my head.

"Silent Hunter, the coast is clear," Linda's voice came out of my earpiece.

I cursed; I was now hands-deep in my work. Literally.

"Silent is working on tonight's barbeque at the moment, I can take a message and get back to you in five?"

"He did it again, didn't he?" Linda asked.

Jess's reply was a giggle into the headset. I finished quickly, saving the organs I normally would, leaving the rest. Since I didn't want to walk around bloody the rest of the day, I took the beast by its front legs and dragged it back. Jessica watched as I pulled, huffing. I was nearly out of breath getting it to the back of the truck. The rut would be starting soon, and this was a large buck, in the prime of his life. Or... former life. I was able to get the tailgate down and half the deer in before Jessica slung her rifle and grabbed the backside and gave it a heave.

It slid in and I pulled it to the back of the cab, then hopped out. Jessica closed the tailgate for me, while I washed my hands off in a puddle on the side of the road. It didn't clean it so much as get the blood off of me. I dried my hands on my pant legs and then put my rifle in the truck, climbing in after it. Once Jess was in, I fired up the truck. She kept her rifle between her knees, the barrel pointing out the window, but her hand was on her pistol, in case of trouble.

THIS STASH WAS LOCATED IN A BARN AS WELL, BUT IT hadn't been an old tumbled down barn. This one had been rebuilt sometime in the last decade. The trailer was in the back, pulled into an old livestock stall. I was able to back the truck into it. Linda and Jay were already halfway unloading it. It was an old U-Haul trailer, with the lettering removed but still visible by the different colors in the paint. I grinned and hopped out, dropping the tailgate.

"When you set out to get food, you don't mess

around," Jay said with a grin, noting the buck in the back.

"I try not to," I agreed.

With four of us working together, we unloaded and reloaded the contents quickly. It filled the bed of the truck to capacity, and I was worried how those riding in the back would be able to sit safely, but Linda shushed my objections and climbed up on the pile.

"This is food is badly needed by our group," she said with a grin. "I don't mind riding back here."

"I don't either," Jay said, "besides, I'm already drooling at the thought of your barbeque skills."

"How did the trap go?" I asked him.

"Same as last one. The door opens, boom. Pretty easy. Going to rig the next one a bit different. Hopefully we'll have some empty boxes of this stuff to repack and use as decoys in case they become suspicious."

"How nefarious of you," Jessica said with a grin. "And thanks, my stomach is giving me trouble this morning."

"Any time. Besides, gives you two some time to talk." He grinned.

WE PULLED INTO GRANDMA'S PROPERTY AND BACKED THE truck up. Linda and Jay hopped out as both Jessica and I got out. Lester walked to us smiling, though his grin went up to his ears when he saw the fat buck I'd shot.

"I'll get some folks unloading this," he told us. I nodded and clapped him on the shoulder. "Remember, we're keeping this one close to the chest, at least where we're getting this stuff. We're still worried about leaks," I told him softly in his ear.

"Understood," he replied, as a small crowd gathered to see what we'd brought back.

"Take my Suburban this time," he said, pressing his keys into my hand.

I hesitated, wondering why. We had another truck staged and ready.

"But..."

"Up to you," he said with a grin, "might throw off people watching us if they always see trucks going out empty and coming back full."

I nodded, and Linda grinned.

"Let me rinse my hands off better first," I told them all.

"Don't get my seats bloody if you kill another one!" Lester called as I walked to the pump.

Jay headed into the barn, to get another set of charges I thought, and Linda and Jessica followed me to the pump.

"Is that food for us?" Melinda, Lester's new paramour asked.

"Yes," I told her. "Food for the entire group."

"There's a few of us who were wondering... The last load of food like that went into one of the rooms and was locked up..."

"Yes, and it's brought out and cooked or distributed at mealtimes," Linda told her.

"The food isn't enough though," another older lady said, standing just behind Melinda.

"You mean it's not as much as you were used to?" Linda asked her.

"No, not even close."

She was one who'd come in with the second group, the ones who'd been a part of the slave revolt.

"It's what we have for now," I told her.

"I don't see you going hungry," one of the younger men said.

"No? I've lost quite a bit of weight. If you'd been here when the lights first went out, you'd notice it," I shot back, feeling defensive.

"Yeah, he probably has his own stash of food," another said.

"If *I* had my *own* stash ... implying that it was already mine? Am I hearing this right?" I asked the third.

"Well ... yeah," the young man said, looking down at his feet.

"If you're unhappy with how the group is providing for you, how the work is divided, nobody is holding you here." I tried to sound compassionate, but it was hard to keep the bitterness out of my voice.

"I don't see *you* in the gardens," the woman with Melinda said, pointing at me as Jay walked up to us, a box in his hands.

"Who did you think put those in originally?" I

asked her. "Me, my Grandma and Grandpa, who, by the way died, protecting people here from getting machine gunned down." This time I didn't hold back the pain and hurt in my voice. Was I overreacting? Being overly sensitive?

"Wes don't let it get to you," Jessica said, putting a hand on my shoulder lightly.

"I'm sorry, but I've sacrificed a lot for these people. I know there's always a few ingrates who were used to ordering fast food, or going out to eat every day who are going to complain, but when they imply that me and my family are not doing our fair share, that we haven't sacrificed—"

Jay stepped forward and interrupted. "Wes and his Grandma have given us a place to live. Some folks came here with what they could. Some were better prepared than others. Some came with nothing. If you've had a meal at all in the last twenty-four-hour period, you're probably luckier than most in this country right now. If you're going to be a bunch of uppity whiney little complainers, how about you shut up?" Jay said, some heat in his voice. "I mean, Mrs. Wexler," he said addressing the woman who'd been standing behind Melinda, "What would that Spider fellow do with you? I could tell you, but I don't think you'd like to hear what I think."

"I... I didn't mean... I'm sorry," she said, and turned to leave, her head down.

Jay wasn't done, however. "Melinda, you've always been a holy roller, showing up for church every

Sunday. Not once did I see you helping in the kitchens, not once did I see you coming in with food during the potlucks we held. You have no room to talk." Then he turned to the young man. "Colton, you're lucky you're not in jail. If it wasn't for your father being State Police and pulling strings, you would have done time for that little joyride with that case of beer. By the way, how old was the girl? The one who was in the stolen truck you crashed?"

"I didn't know she wasn't an adult," he said angrily. "And as soon as I found out, I broke it off!" He was pissed, but not enough to take a swing.

I was really starting to like Jay. The small crowd murmured as people talked.

"I'm happy to have a place, warm food to eat. I didn't come here with a lot of supplies, but you don't hear me complaining," another young man said to murmurs of agreement.

"Let's go," Linda said, rolling her eyes, her tone icy.

17

TWO MORE STOPS, two more traps. We'd pushed our luck as we could that day.

Jay went back to the barn for the night, while the rest of us sat on the porch.

"You know they're just scared," Grandma told me.

We'd been discussing what had gone on earlier.

"I know," I told her, "but the rumors still bug me, and I don't know what to do about them."

"Maybe we should do townhall meetings?" Linda suggested.

"I don't dislike that idea," I told her, "but wasn't that how Henry got the bulk of the group to go along with whatever he wanted?"

Jessica winced, but it had to be said.

"Yeah, it was. If it had been done properly, I don't think he would have been able to pull what he did though. You're not Henry, for what it's worth."

"That's what I'm worried about, that somehow

Grandma and I are..." I let my words trail off as I thought about how to express what I was feeling, "like we have the final veto, or vote, and none of what they think matters."

"But we do have the final veto," Grandma protested. "This is our damned property. Actually, it's yours, according to the county."

"What?" I asked her, turning to her in shock.

"Grandpa did up the paperwork when he found out about the cancer," Grandma told her. "It's in the locked box at the bank. If something were to happen to him, he was leaving it to you."

"But... I don't understand?"

"It's what he wanted," Grandma said. "He knew you'd always take care of me if he didn't... if the treatment didn't work. Said unless we did it, it'd get tied up in the courts somehow, especially if your mother ever came back in the picture." The last was said quietly.

I took a sip of lemonade, the un-doctored kind that came from a premixed package.

Jessica's hand found mine and we thought about that as we sat on the steps. Curt and Lester were in the chairs we'd left open, with Grandma in her rocker.

"It makes sense," Linda said at last. "Lots of trusts and wills are set up like that, Wes."

"Sorry, but not to derail things, but I don't even know—"

"I knew about it as well," Lester told me. "And let's be honest, even if I took all the complainers back to my place, there'd be no room to grow additional crops there. Sure, we could hunt game, but as you've seen, it's getting hunted out around here. That big buck you bagged today was at the far edges of where the people are concentrated. I'm sure there's pockets of onesies and twosies, but if they are hunting for dinner, they're cutting down game and probably spooking a ton of it out of the area as well."

I mulled on that.

"What do you suggest?" I asked everyone, since they all seemed to be looking at me.

"Keep doing what you are doing," Curt told me. "From what I've seen, your family has lived on less than everyone here, yet you've done well for yourselves before and after things went to shit."

"I can second that," Lester said, "and a lot of it was your work, Wes. You'd find a diamond, or help your grandpa in the shine room..."

"You created opportunities where there weren't many options," Curt said before I could respond.

"And the legend grows!" Jess said, giggling.

I poked her in the side, making her squeak, then pulled her close to me, kissing her gently.

"Stop with that. These rumors bug me," I told her gently.

"I know, but you're this mysterious outlaw. You're like Billy the Kid mixed with Popcorn Sutton," she was smiling, our faces close.

"Am not," I told her, "Billy the Kid was a bank robber."

"A good shot though," Linda said. "How many do you usually fire when you're hunting?"

"You all can kiss my white a—"

"You're not too old to spank," Grandma interrupted, which made the folks already chuckling at our back and forth howl with laughter.

"I wonder," I said after we all quieted, "if this is what the group is missing? The comradery, the back and forth?"

"There's groups within groups here," Lester told me. "Some of the ladies stick together, some moms and their kids stick together, the cops kinda stick close to the other cops. I mean, when it's all chow time, everyone comes to the stewpot with their bowls and spoons at the end of the day."

I had a thought and went inside. I grabbed two half gallon glass carboys that I'd put in the pantry. They were what I'd stored some proofed 'shine in for drinking. I checked the caps to make sure I wasn't about to hand out 180 proof, then headed out. Everyone saw that and Lester broke out into a grin.

"Going to share some of that with us?" he asked.

"I think I'm going to share some with everyone," I told him. "If they brought their bowls, hopefully they brought their cups too!"

Jessica got up from the steps and took one of the jugs in her left hand and held her right one out to me. I took her hand in my left and we walked down the steps. A moment later, I heard the porch steps creaking and everyone including Grandma were following us.

"Where's the dogs?" I asked Jessica.

"Emily and Mary were playing fetch with them, working out some of their energy. If they're done, they're probably inside the barn. They like to sleep on the hay in the shine room."

"You liked sleeping on the hay in the shine room," I teased her, watching her turn red in the face.

"I remember that morning!" Grandma said laughing. "I hadn't seen my grandson buck-ass naked since he was—"

"Grandma!" I said over my shoulder, "little ears ahead."

The area around the cookfire was raked clean of any chicken mess on an almost daily basis, and the ground was pretty flattened from the backsides of everyone who sat there patiently. Why hadn't I joined them there at the fire? There were too many faces and names I didn't know, yet it seemed everyone knew me, had an opinion of me.

"There he is!" Mary exclaimed from the side of the fire.

Emily was sitting next to her, though as packed as the space around the fire was, people kept their distance from her a bit. There was enough room for Jessica and the rest of us to sit. I did and looked around. Some people were talking in groups, some were tucking into the thick stew that had been cooked, and there was a second batch going on the fire for those who worked the late shift watching and protecting us.

"Evening folks, mind if we join you?" I asked.

Murmurs of welcome greeted us, and I sat.

"Figured I'd join everyone for a little bit," I told them.

"And the big chief has brought firewater!" Emily said loudly, to more than a few guffaws of laughter from the nearly forty people sitting there.

"I ran some of this a bit back if you'll remember. Now I personally like to let it sit a while, to age and mellow, but times being what they are ... you won't mind if this isn't my usual quality?"

"Hell no! I haven't had a drink in months!" a man in the back called.

"Well, pass this one around," I said handing the jug to Emily, who passed it on. "Use your cups if you can, and make sure none of the younglings get into it."

OUR CORE GROUP TALKED AROUND THE FIRE. NOT ABOUT anything that would be hurtful to us if it got back to Spider, but our banter was interrupted with questions from time to time. We included everyone who wanted to talk to us, long into the night. A lot of the questions were directed at me and Jess, then Linda. There was a lot of curiosity about the survival group they both had been in.

A lot of questions were about our families' moonshining days, which Grandma and I only talked about in half-truths. At some point, one of the men walked to the porch and brought her rocker down, which she greatly appreciated.

"So, what got you interested in preparing for a big disaster?" Mrs. Wexler asked.

"Mostly seeing what happened with Katrina and reading about how unprepared most people were for a big disaster. It put things in perspective for me, about how really fragile life here is. We've lived most of our lives below the poverty line, doing what we had to, to survive already. One major blow, and we'd be wiped out financially. There were some years where we had to take..." I looked around the group suspiciously, hamming it up, "deer out of season, because we had to pay the bills and didn't have the money for food."

"Don't worry, no 'possum sheriff's around here!" Lester said with a grin.

We were deep into the second half gallon of moonshine, everyone taking a shot or sip of it here and there. There were a lot of folks who thought it was a bit strong for their tastes, but there were almost as many who held their cups up for more.

"Just being a smartass," I told him, to some chuckles. "Besides, we've all broken the law in one way or another since the collapse."

People fell silent and looked up at me. With a start, I realized that I had almost everyone's attention with that statement.

"I mean, look at how many of us are armed, and with guns that used to be illegal. I've taken to carrying an M4 with an unlicensed suppressor, same with my pistol. We've killed game out of season, a lot of us stayed behind and didn't get packed into cattle cars and sent to centers with the rest of the folks in the area went into. Just by being here, and being armed, we're *all* breaking the law, according to the last executive order I heard over the radio."

"Hell, I have that laminated copy your Grandpa had of it," Grandma said loudly, "and he's right. There're laws on the books that make no sense. We're not hunting game into extinction, we're not hurting anybody who comes around here who don't want to hurt us first, and by golly, I love me some untaxed corn liquor." Grandma held her cup up, and I poured for her.

Melinda and Mrs. Wexler smiled at that, but the smile didn't reach their eyes. Judgie little ladies. Those two were probably the types that Grandpa warned me about. Every day but Sunday, they probably sat in their parlor, binoculars in hand, to see all the latest gossip about. Busybodies.

"If we're breaking casual laws," Jay said, "how bad do you think those other groups are out there doing things?"

The jolly mood sort of died with those words.

"Sometimes, there's some people that just need to be stopped," Lester said simply, taking a sip. "There's breaking casual laws, and there's breaking major and moral ones. What Spider's doing is an abomination."

"So, what are we going to do about that?" the man who'd first shouted earlier asked.

"We're working on a response. Right now, I have to keep things close to the vest."

"Why?" he called back.

"Because, we never know who is listening and reporting back to the other side," I said simply.

More silence.

"I don't know about you guys and gals," Jessica said getting up and brushing off her backside, "but I'm bushed. Wes?"

I stood and took her hand; Emily had left earlier with a sleeping Mary. I whistled low, and a few moments later the dogs showed up. Raider sniffed my hand and then rubbed his head against my leg affectionately.

"I'm ready. You folks have a nice night. Save those carboys for me, so if I get a chance, I can fill them back up and we'll all do this again."

"I think I'm headed in too, Curt," Margie said, pulling on her husband's hand.

"Lester?" Melinda asked, an eyebrow raised.

"I think we're going to take a walk," Les told me. "Night folks!"

We said our goodbyes and headed into the house. Diesel had run ahead of us when we'd gone inside and when Jessica and I got to the bedroom, he was already sprawled across the bed. Jessica sighed, and ordered him down. He responded by snoring.

"Diesel, don't you play that game with me," Jessica said, not quite stamping her foot.

He lifted his head and looked at her, then the dog lifted his stubby tail and farted loudly.

"I think I'm going to take the couch," I told her, pulling on her hand.

"Yeah…"

We went to the living room to see Raider and Yaeger on the floor near the wood stove, almost nose to nose, playing gently, using front paws and gentle nips. I grinned at that and sat in my spot. Jessica settled in on my lap and leaned back, pulling the lightweight afghan over us.

"That was a good idea tonight," Jessica said.

"Pure luck," I whispered to her.

"Pure inspiration. You made yourself a human in front of them. Not some supernatural being."

"I'm anything but supernatural," I said, feeling the strain, and the exhaustion and comfort of having Jessica snuggled in so tight made my eyes heavy.

"You are exceptional, however." She kissed my arm around her left shoulder.

"I love you, silly woman."

"Is your Grandma asleep?" she asked, turning on the couch slightly.

"With her earplugs in probably, I told her, feeling the sleepiness leave me suddenly.

"Good."

18

"You guys and gals ready to go?" I asked the group standing around a truck we hadn't used yet for the raiding of the stolen FEMA supplies.

"Ready to roll," Linda said, hopping into the back of the truck.

"You want to drive?" I asked Jessica.

"No, I like being chauffeured around. Makes me feel like a princess," she snarked, dropping me a wink.

"Looks like I'm riding bitch again," Jay said with a grin.

"You want to drive?" I asked him.

"No, I'm ok," he said, looking at Linda out of the side of his eye.

I grinned. She was getting a lot of attention from the men lately. First Michael, and now Jay? Maybe I was reading too much into it.

We loaded up, this time with the spare trailer in tow. It would be hell on us if we had to maneuver fast, but we could hit twice as many places before heading back to the homestead. We were worried all the extra movement would draw more attention. I was sure we were being watched and that they'd see we had a trailer, but there had to be a ton of these all over the state. The risk of less exposure outweighed my wariness, so I'd suggested it, and laid out my reasons for the group to debate. I was expecting pushback but got none.

"It's short enough to shoot over, but if we drop into the bed, it'll help be a bullet stop," was all Linda had told us.

"Sound logic to me. The more of these we hit, sooner or later it'll get out to Spider," Jay had said. "Besides, it'll be less eyes seeing us coming and going. They won't know exactly what we've done unless they're following us."

"I like it the idea," Jessica had said.

That was how I found myself driving slower, feeling the ass end of this truck wanting to go sideways down the chatter bumps of an old dirt road in the South West side of the county. One thing I couldn't tell from the maps, but was becoming apparent now, was that the stashes we'd hit so far had all come from very rural out of the way places. Not where you'd expect to find a king's ransom worth of food, medicines (as we'd found in yesterday's last stop) and supplies.

"You know," I told Jessica quietly, "I think Jay's got the hots for your mom."

"You noticed that too?" she asked sweetly. "When did it come to you?"

"About twenty minutes ago," I told her, slowing to find a good place to pull off the road so they could scout up ahead.

"Hm. Still slow as usual." She smiled when she said it, but I barely held back an eye roll and a groan.

"Doesn't that bug you?" I asked her.

"My mom's been pretty her whole life," Jessica said. "I kinda know the signs. I'm sure you even checked her out a time or two."

"Did not," I shot back.

"Oh, come on," she said, still teasing, as I found a wide spot in the road, around a curve that was perfect and pulled in.

"Maybe before we were dating," I told her. "Just curious to see what you'd look like in twenty or thirty years, so not really checking her out."

"What??" She slapped my arm.

"Hey, you asked," I told her, rubbing my arm, then turning off the motor.

"You two keep the noise down," Linda said, hopping out of the truck.

I got out to see she was smiling, and Jay's face was beet red.

"We will," I told her.

Jay flipped me off good-naturedly, and started walking quickly with Linda, until they were quickly out of sight.

"Think they heard us?" I asked Jessica.

"Probably," she said with a sigh. "Let's go find a spot to sit and wait."

"Ok, how's your stomach?" I asked her.

"How's your head?" she asked.

"I wasn't drinking last night."

"Sure...."

"Come on," I said, groaning. "I'm still sick to my stomach thinking about that last hangover. I don't think I've ever tied one on like that before."

"You know, I don't mind if you do drink. Just... People saw you down a better part of a jug that night and go staggering in. Kind of ... amazed ... that somebody could still function after all that booze."

"I had a two-day hangover," I pointed out.

She laughed, remembering. "Over here!"

She pointed and I nodded. Further to the left, there was an old tree that had blown over, probably in a storm in the last few years. It hadn't rotted, but it'd make a good spot to sit behind, and give us cover, yet it wasn't too large to see over.

"We have movement at the stash," Jay's voice came in over the radio. "I see two figures coming in and out of a lean-to."

"I've got three on my side,' Linda said into my earpiece.

Jess cursed.

"Regulars?" I asked.

"Black vests. Pretty sure I see KGR patches on at least two," Linda said.

"See any backup?" Jessica asked.

"Two of the three I see are in hiding positions, watching things. Third seems to be patrolling. Sounds like Jaybird's two are loading a vehicle?"

"Correct," Jay said.

"Do we take them out?" I asked her.

"Risky either way," Linda said quietly, almost a whisper coming out of the radio. "We let them take this, the team might not show up if they hit another stash we trapped. Or we take them now and take the supplies... or we do nothing and get nothing."

"I like the options where the KGR's die," I said softly.

Jessica put her hand on my arm. "Don't be so bloodthirsty," she whispered to me, not the radio.

"Eight o'clock Green," Linda's voice said, "Come in Six White."

"Copy," I said softly. "Ok, I'm sure you know what that means better than I do," I said to Jessica who grinned and nodded.

LINDA HAD MOVED OFF FORTY YARDS FROM JAY'S position and was under her own camo netting. I hadn't brought mine, so I stayed low to the ground, the unmown ditches and weeds providing plenty of cover. I wasn't wearing blaze orange, but my shirt wouldn't stand out much if I sat up. Jessica had moved in near her mother as well. The whispered plan over the radio was simple. Linda and I had suppressed weapons.

Jessica would cover our backsides, while Jay could provide crossfire if anybody broke away or tried to sneak up on us. We were going to hit them, wait, and then move in and loot. What could go wrong?

"I've got the two watchers in sight," Linda whispered.

"I've got angles on all three. Who's your target?" I asked, seeing the men in camouflage hunkering down and waiting, though their black vests stood out.

"I'll take the first on the left," Linda whispered back.

"I'll take the second one, then work on the ones loading the trucks."

"Likewise," Linda said. "Girl Scout and Jaybird, ready?"

"Three count?" Jay asked.

"Sounds good," Linda said back, "One, Two, Three."

Both of us fired at once at the three count. It wasn't a particularly difficult shot for me, and I saw my bullet take my man in the back of the head, tumbling him over. I trusted Linda's to do the same. I was already scanning for the men loading. I didn't want to take one down and have the other bolt, so I took a deep cleansing breath and waited until I saw both. One had just put a box in the back of the truck to turn when I gently squeezed the trigger. I heard Linda's gun go off half a heartbeat after my shot, but I was scanning for the second man.

"What the—" I heard him exclaim and moved my

rifle slightly, seeing the man turn to look at the man I'd hit in the side of the neck when I took my next shot.

It had been hurried and not as aimed and hit him in the vest. I cursed as he was went down, clutching at where I'd hit him. I put another shot downrange, and this one missed his head to the right. I had to move. I stood and started jogging, trying to close the gap and get a better angle.

"Report?" Jay asked.

"Four down, one wounded, Silent is moving in, all cover Silent Hunter," Jessica hissed.

It bothered me that the killing didn't bother me. My mind was racing, but that thought swirled in the background paranoia that had been building, like a snowball rolling downhill, picking up mass and speed as it went. The man I'd shot saw me coming and started rising, his hand going for a pistol. I flicked the switch on my M4 to PEW PEW PEW and fired a burst. Three geysers of dirt erupted as he cleared leather. I fired again.

I didn't know which rounds, the first or the last, it was that downed him, but the last one took him just above the vest, below the base of the neck, and his head rocked as gore-streaked the ground behind him.

"Target down," I said, coming to a stop, then remembered I hadn't thumbed my radio.

"Target down," Jess said in my earpiece.

I took position in front of the truck, using the front end and engine as cover. We had watched them for a while and were fairly confident there had only been five.

"Damn good shooting for a civvy," Jay said in the radio.

"Thanks," I replied, remembering to hit the mic button, then put my rifle on safe to wait.

"CHARLIE TEAM, REPORT," THE VOICE CAME OUT OF ONE of the radio's we'd scavenged off the bodies, this one from the first lookout Linda had popped.

"Don't answer," Linda said told Jessica, who was holding onto it.

We'd almost finished loading the trucks and I was going through the gear we'd scavenged. It would go back to the homestead, where the vests would be cleaned up and spray painted a matte green, so we didn't take friendly fire in the heat of the moment, something even the police in our group had started to do, despite their hesitation to deface their gear.

It wasn't much gear compared to what I'd been expecting. There were rifles, handguns, couple of spare magazines each and the vest I'd shot was pretty much ruined, but the rest were fine, if not a little bloody. I'd debated taking the boots, but I hadn't. I knew some-where somebody would probably second guess this, but I didn't want some dude's foot fungus to leap to one of our folks.

"What should we do with the bodies?" I asked them.

"I was thinking of dragging them into the trailer, setting the trap, then leaving them," Jay said immediately.

"I like that idea," Jess and Linda chorused.

I shook my head and got my hands on the dead man's legs and started dragging him towards the trailer. It took us twenty sweaty minutes of work, but then the grisly task was done. The radio calls for the dead men were becoming more frequent and it was becoming apparent to me that they would probably send another team out to check on them.

"What about the truck?" I asked.

"Take it or leave it?" Jay asked the ladies.

"Go ahead and drive it back home," Linda told him. "It's something familiar to them, maybe we can use it some time."

"I think we've worn out our welcome here anyway. I think we're pushing our luck trying to get any more food drops today. If they can't find the men, they'll probably search the trailers. We don't know how many of them they were supposed to hit today," Jessica said.

I nodded in agreement. It was time to go. Hopefully Michael could use these new radios to predict and break the next set of codes when they changed them. In the meantime, we had overstayed here way too long.

19

———

WE DECIDED to lay low the next couple of days. Linda and Michael were scanning radio frequencies, and listening to Spider's men report in - or not report in. Several teams had gone looking for the missing men. Our decision to cut short our plans of nabbing food had paid off. I left Linda and Michael in the barn to find Sheriff Jackson and Deputy Rolston waiting near the water pump.

"Got a second?" The Sheriff asked.

"Sure," I told him, both of them looking like the cats who had just ate the canary. Raider was walking between the men, his tail wagging furiously.

"Remember that hog that the little girl... DJ ... said she saw?" Rolston asked.

"Yeah?"

"Sounds like the same group or another group of hogs are in the wild areas behind your property..."

"I haven't ever heard of them being around here,

but it's worth a shot. You want me to organize some way to make bacon?" I asked them, grinning.

"Listen, we can all hunt here, but we haven't on those guys, because they're nocturnal and avoid people, but what if we were to lay into some meat? What do you think about building a big smoker to preserve some of it?"

"I really like that idea," I told him simply. "We'd have to scavenge for supplies, make it..."

I broke off because Rolston looked like he was about to burst out of his britches. He had an idea, and by the look on his face it was a really good one. I pointed at him, while he had a hand down to pet Raider's head.

"That little covered old U-Haul trailer?" he asked.

"Yeah?"

"What if we cut a round hole through the floor near the rear doors where it's easy to get to. We can bury pipe and make a covered fire a little down the hill from it. Let the bad weather stripping on the rear doors work as vents. In case of an emergency, we just hook up to it with one of the trucks and drive off."

"What would we hang the meat from?" I asked him.

"Remember those sections of cattle panel?" the sheriff asked me.

I started grinning, nodding my head. Raider caught scent of something and went to investigate. Foghorn? Where was that old bird?

"I measured inside of the trailer. Where the curved

top meets the straight walls there's a lip where the two sections are riveted together. The hole cut through the floor would really be the only work to do to convert it, other than trimming the cattle panels to fit..."

"I like it," I told them grinning. "We'll probably have to do it in front of the house, or back behind the main garden where the hill slopes down."

"I was thinking about behind the garden," Sheriff Jackson said, "although I am curious about another garden I found."

"What do you mean?" I asked him, confused, thinking of smoked ham, smoked bacon, pork chops...

"Got you some green growing in the very back of the property," Rolston said with a grin.

Duh!

"Oh yeah," I said sheepishly, "I sorta forgot about that with everything going on. "Grandma put those in. She originally said maybe we could use something like that to trade with Spider's guys to stay away from us... But she knew my Grandpa's cancer was coming back. I didn't see it at first, but looking back..."

My words trailed off, and I felt sick at the memory of finding my Grandma holding onto his lifeless body.

Raider came back, nose still close to the ground and stopped at my feet. I pet him, my pup leaning into me so I could scratch between his shoulder blades.

"Oh," Sheriff Jackson said softly, "I thought it was another business or something."

"Not one of mine," I told him honestly. "My

grandma had seeds from the time my mom was still around."

Rolston looked at his uncle. "Liz Flagg was a hellion on two wheels," he turned to me, "sorry," then turned back to Rolston. "When she wound up pregnant, she settled down some, but when the boy here was oh ... a year and a half, two years old?... she up and left. Got herself back involved with a bad crowd. Headed to the west coast on the back of a motorcycle. She'd show up once in a while, but always kept away from Wes here."

"Wait, what?" I asked him, shocked he even knew my mother's name.

"You've got to remember son, I've been with the Sheriff's department almost longer than you've been alive, maybe longer. I remember her, she's probably close to my age, but I don't really remember."

"How did ... but you knew her?" I asked.

His eyes twinkled. "Wanted to know her back in the day. Beautiful woman, opinionated, and boy could she curse the bark right off a tree if she took a mind to... But no, not really. When a small town has a lady like your mother in it, everybody notices."

"Is that a good thing, or a bad thing?" I almost hated to ask, but not knowing who my father was, I had no idea what kind of information I was about to get. Was she the town...?

"Oh, both I imagine. She really woke the teachers in the schools, kept the local police here on their toes.

She'd walk into a room, and everybody would stop. It was to either look at how pretty she was, or to wait and see what came out of her mouth next. That woman had sass, and more than a few fellows were heartbroken when she left town. Missed their chance to ask her out."

He meant him? I'd have to ask Grandma, but I supposed it made sense why the sheriff knew my grandparents. Didn't it? Rolston gave me a wan smile and a shrug.

"I ... anyway, that's why the weed is back there. Think it's something we have to keep the little ones away from?" I asked.

"Naw but having it around for... situations like what your grandpa was going through... as much as it pains me to say it, I think it wouldn't hurt anybody. We'll just make sure none of the kids and younger teenagers try to sneak out there. Actually, we should keep some of the older two-legged kids away also," he said, pointing to Rolston.

"Me?" he asked, both hands in the air.

"I remember getting the phone call. You were in your mommas' garage, in that old lazy boy. She said she found two roaches and you reeking... talking about how modern day tap dance was—"

"Uncle Will!" Rolston said quickly, "let's forget that ever happened. Must have been something more in the ... oh hell!" He flipped his uncle off, who pushed him gently while we both laughed.

Raider let his tongue hang out, sharing the joke. Dang, he was getting sharper and sharper all the time.

"Ok, so if you want to take care of modifying the trailer, I'll see if I can scare up a couple of guys and let's see what we can do about getting some pork on the menu again!"

"That sounds like a great plan!"

COLTON, MARSHALL AND TWO YOUNGER TEENS, Brandon and Anthony, joined me. There was a small crowd gathering around the stall as I showed them how I made my snares. A while back I'd bought some large spools of snare wire. Most of it was lightweight, but I had the heavier cable for the times I was going after deer. Most of the time I didn't use it for that, preferring to shoot them, but if I could teach these guys how to provide meat without having to fire off a shot, it would take some pressure off of me... and the undercurrent of fear; fear of not having enough food.

"So, after you put it through the camlock..." Colton said.

"Yeah, then you crimp the ends. See how it pulls tight?" I asked him, letting the loop close on my left hand. "It won't give any slack until you release the lock like this," I showed them.

"What happens if it doesn't go around their necks?" Marshall asked. "Gets their foot or something?"

"Depends, I guess. You could always shoot them if they're still in the wire," I told him.

"I like that. Don't they see the wire, though?" Brandon asked.

"They probably will, but like deer, these guys are used to pushing through the brush with their head. They won't realize it's a trap until they're down."

"Can I make the next one?" Anthony asked.

"Sure," I told him stepping back.

We'd made a few large snares for hogs, and I got the supplies out to start making snares for smaller game. "But we have to keep the dogs away from these. They'll kill without caring what kind of creature gets into them."

Raider made a sound, his head brushing against my leg. I scratched at his back, before he flopped down at my feet.

"Which means you'll have to stick close to me while the snares are out," I told him, "and Yaeger and Diesel too."

"He doesn't go very far away from people when he isn't with you," Brandon said.

"Yeah, but if he were tracking or scenting something... Better safe than sorry. Besides, if you guys want to do this, you're going to want to check the traps at least once a day."

"Twice a day if I can," Marshall said rubbing his stomach. "That last pig tasted a little funny, but I haven't had any in so long it didn't bother me. Like having pineapple on your pizza delivered by accident. You don't like it, but you eat it."

"Pineapple on pizza is an abomination," Colton told him.

"I wholeheartedly agree; pineapple should never go on pizza."

"Why not?" Jess asked, walking in, her two pups pushing through the small group standing outside so they could be with their mom.

"Because it's disgusting," I told her.

"Peanut butter and pickles?" she asked, an eyebrow raised.

"Yuck," Marshall said.

Diesel woofed, but I didn't know if he was agreeing, or acknowledging we were talking about food. The dog was smart, but sometimes I didn't think he was on the same level as our shepherds.

"When we put these out, we're going to have to keep the dogs away," I told Jessica. "We'll have to set them a lot lower than we did for the deer."

Jessica walked over to one of the cables and picked it up, whistling and patting her leg. Raider walked over and sat in front of her, as the other two dogs fell into line with him, all three now sitting at attention. She held it out, so they sniffed, then she said something in either German or Hungarian that made the dogs flinch and pull back. She put the snare behind her back and waited until they'd gotten over whatever it was she'd told them. She hadn't stopped training with Raider since moving in here, she'd just not included me in everything.

"Stay," she said, and brought the wire back out again and held it out to the dogs.

Raider leaned forward to sniff, but when she repeated the words, he flinched back. Again, she put it behind her back. A couple moments later she was holding it back out in front of her. The dogs turned their heads, not wanting to get close to it, not meeting her eyes. Jessica tossed it over the dog's heads and back to me. I caught it and put it in the pile.

"We'll have to keep working with them, but they have the general idea for now. Repetition and reward will help them pick up on it fast. Still, we need to be careful."

"Agreed," I said. "You going hunting with us?"

"Sure, but let's leave the dogs here," she told me.

"That'd be great," Marshall said, eyeballing Diesel.

"Oh, don't worry Marshall, he's not like Yaeger and Raider here. He won't eat somebody unless I tell him to, and he thinks you're his buddy."

"Oh good, I just … he's so big."

"Want to pet him, before we all head out and I have to put them up?"

"I … no thanks. Not yet. Sort of gotten used to Raider. Took me a while, but..."

"It's ok, buddy," she said, putting one hand on his arm. "I'm going to run these three in. I think Emily is making Mary and Grandma lunch, they'll watch them for us."

"You think Emily will want to learn this?" I asked her.

"I'll ask," Jessica said. Raider barked once, his tongue hanging out the side of his mouth.

"Yes, we know you like Emily most of the time," I told him, "you little traitor."

20

THE WALK to the back of the property didn't take all that long. I had my rifle with me, with the suppressor off and regular ammunition loaded in it as a just in case. I wasn't expecting to need it, but better safe than sorry, and I needed to clean it. I'd used it and let it sit, not knowing how corrosive the powder was that Les had used ... a project for tonight maybe.

"What's to stop them from not using that trail?" Marshall asked.

"Nothing, but all critters like to go the path of least resistance. So that's why we put this loop on this game trail, about fifteen inches up."

"What if we pushed sticks in the ground, sort of funneling them into the loop?" Anthony asked.

"Get your smell all over the place, dumbass," Brandon said.

"Animals don't always associate human smells with danger," I told them. "Besides, this might be around for a few days before it sees any action. But in general, it's a good idea," I told them.

Anthony flipped off Brandon, a smug look on his face, as Brandon looked like he was considering making a wrestling match out of things. In the end, Jessica raised an eyebrow and they settled. Colton and Marshall looked amused, but were watchful.

"Ok, so how many more do we have?" Marshall asked.

We'd put out some small game snares on smaller trails already, but after walking, we'd found a trail that had the mark of what I thought might be pig activity, something I hadn't seen much of, ever.

"Five more," I said pulling out some orange marking tape I had in my backpack.

I ripped a length off and tied it off on a tree limb above my head. "Now, if you were hunting and trapping out of season, you wouldn't want to mark a trap like this. It'd be a red flag to the Possum sheriffs," I said.

"What's that?" Colton asked, "I've heard you use that before but..."

"Game Wardens," Jessica answered before I could. "The guys checking your licenses for fishing, trapping and hunting?"

"Oh, those guys? Gotcha. Because what we're doing isn't exactly legal?"

"No, not really," I told him. "But I don't think killing feral hogs would hurt anybody's feelings. They're supposed to be really wild, and there's a ton of them.

No bag limits, but a snare set for a hog could easily get a younger deer, a dog ... you know?"

"Aren't snares illegal?" Jessica asked me.

"You know, I never stopped to check," I told her with a grin, "because I was gonna do it anyway."

"That's what I'm talking about," Brandon said with a grin.

We set the rest of them out. Marshall and Colton promised to check them daily, and one of them would always have a gun to dispatch something if they got larger game. They knew to bring the trap wire back with the game so I could see if we could re-use it, or just parts of it. The camlocks were definitely reusable, but the crimped ends and wire generally took a beating. That was why it was made out of inexpensive materials.

We debated the legalities and moralities of what we were doing, and how all of that changed in a pure survival situation, and I was surprised to hear Colton being the voice of reason for the guys younger than Marshall. I noted that they kind of looked up to him. What Jay had said about the young guy bothered me a bit though, so when we got close, I tapped him on the shoulder and nodded my head off to the side.

"You guys go on ahead, I'm going to be a second," I told them.

Jessica stayed near me, which is what I figured she would do. We watched the other guys walking back, and even Marshall was joking with the younger guys.

"Listen, I didn't mean to jump your shit the other day—"

"I'm not mad about that," I told him, "and honestly, things were getting ready to come to a boil. It happened and it's over. What I wanted to know about was that stolen truck and the girl."

He looked down, his face flushing in anger. "I was stupid. Drunk with some buddies. Somebody dared me to take one of my dad's bowling buddies' trucks. I was originally going to drive it around and park it somewhere else like a prank but..."

He looked up and met my eyes, "See, I'd met this gal named Brenda. I didn't know she was seventeen, I swear, she told me she was twenty."

"Go on," I said.

"Anyway, she asked if we could get some beers before we parked the truck. So, I thought sure, I was going to score you know? And we got them and when I was driving the truck to where we were going to park it across the street, she starts pulling my shirt up, untucking it from my jeans?" The last bit was embarrassing him, and he looked at Jessica once, quickly.

"Then I crashed. I mean, that's what happened. I was an idiot, I never should have done it, but Brenda didn't look seventeen. You know? What are you supposed to do when a hot girl starts pulling on your clothes ... tell her to show ID? Even if you think she's older than you?"

"I'm not here to judge," I told him quietly, "I was just curious. We've been fighting off those Kegger assholes, and they liked to take what wasn't theirs, including women and children, and it didn't matter what age they were to them."

"That's not something I'd condone either," Colton said softly, "I'm not a kidnapper or rapist either." The last was said with some heat.

"He wasn't saying you were," Jessica said, putting a hand on his forearm to get his attention, "but knowing the story ... with him being the head honcho around here, he kind of wanted to know, since without context it might have looked differently."

"Yeah, I guess I can see what you're talking about, ma'am."

"Don't you ma'am me! I'm only a few years older than you!" She sounded indignant but was smiling.

"Yes ma'am," he said drawing out the last word more than was necessary, "but you being the head honcho's lady, means you're somebody I got to look up to and respect, no matter what."

She dropped her hand to her side, a grin spreading across her face.

"And her legend grows!" I said, putting my hands in the air, giving her the mock applause.

She slugged me in the stomach lightly, and I made a woofing sound Raider would have been proud of, then she walked away, hips swaying, flipping her hair behind her shoulders.

"What was that about?" Colton asked.

"Pregnancy hormones?"

We followed after her, and again Colton promised

to always check the traps, first in the morning and two hours before dark. We didn't want any non-targeted animals to get in there, but I was thinking of coming back in the following days with some of Grandma's scratch corn to sort of bait the traps a bit. I hoped that would work and we could pack in some food before Spider caught on to what we'd done and were going to keep doing.

We still had to flush the traitor out, but I hoped with recent events—getting more food, spreading out the hunting and meat gathering, getting to know everyone and sharing drinks with comradery; I hoped the traitor or traitors would leave on their own. Either way, we were about to flush them out, give Spider a bloody nose, or both at the same time. Soon.

21

IT WAS TIME. That thought sent chills running through me. It was time to flush out the traitor - or traitors. This plan would either work, or it'd fail in a spectacular fashion. Since I was the eternal optimist, I was hoping for it'd work better than we could have ever hoped. We'd assembled the team and read them all in.

Linda had vouched for Michael, the guy who'd been working radio with her. He'd been the one to break the code for us the first time and had their next one cracked already. It also helped that, while he'd been trying to romance Linda, he'd gotten to know the radio systems rather well - if not better than Linda herself. I worried about what he'd overheard from Spider about her and I, but he hadn't believed it; he knew where she'd slept in the barracks portion of the barn. So outside of the four of us going, we had three that knew the plan for sure.

"Where you guys going?" Les called as the ladies

started loading ammunition into magazines in the armory.

"To kick a hornet's nest," I told him. "The sheriff and the deputies have home defense while we're gone."

I was carrying the suppressed AR and had the dump pouch full of a mixture of magazines, my .45, a small backpack full goodies to make sure I was the head shenanigator, and I'd even included the Saran Wrap.

"Good, it's about time we start whittling their numbers down. This a secret?" he asked me, his voice lowering, as he looked around.

"Naw," I told him, "but we don't want to make a fuss going out either. Going to take mom's truck."

"You're taking the spare .50?" he asked.

"Yeah, it's already got a belt on it," I told him.

"Let me get you another couple ammo cans," he said, walking to the wooden crate and hefting two of them out.

"It's a weird day in Arkansas when a little truck gets turned into a 'technical'," he said, huffing past me.

Emily walked in, her lever gun and the BFR strapped to her hip. She'd dressed in a spare camo outfit of Jess's, but she looked like she was drowning in it. She'd pegged her pants into her boots, and her hair was tucked into a camouflage hat of mine I used for hunting.

"Need a hand?" she asked Les sweetly as we headed to the truck.

"No, I'm good," he said, putting both ammo cans in the back of the truck. "When you get back here, check in your rifle and pistol so I can give them a good going over and cleaning."

"Why Lester, you're wanting to fondle my big ... gun?" Emily asked.

The big man blinked and started turning pink. Melinda heard that, as she was walking by with a book in her hand, headed for the sunshine.

"No... I... I've never... I've always wanted one of those. Figured I could check it out, clean it, make sure it's still to spec."

"Ok, no problemo!" Emily said and got on her tiptoes and kissed the old outlaw on his stubbled cheek.

I thought his head was going to pop.

"You're driving," Jessica called, "I've got the most time on the big guns. In case we run into trouble."

"What about the farm?" I asked her.

"Scouts said the workers have cleared out for now. They harvested and replanted."

"At least they're productive," I murmured.

I got in the truck, and Raider whined. I looked out the back window and Jess shrugged.

"Come on boy, you ride up here with me and Linda," I said.

He barked happily and jumped in, barely clearing the gap between my chest and the steering wheel. Linda got in last, slamming the door.

"Why am I riding shotgun?" she asked, the extra-long gun she carried when I'd first met her in the woods propped just out the door.

"Because Emily needs to learn the .50 and how to operate it," I said, firing up the truck.

"And she isn't sitting in the front seat with you," Linda shot back, a grin coming across her face.

"And she isn't sitting in the front seat with me," I agreed.

"We can hear you," Emily called out from the back.

I sighed and started driving out.

22

THE GUYS HAD REMOVED part of the mounts from the burned-out APC, and after thorough cleaning, had it mounted in the back of the truck in the middle of the bed. It looked like a Rube Goldberg affair, but Linda assured me it'd work. Besides, the truck was the perfect size. Or something. I rolled slowly down the road and took the long way. Linda knew where Henry's people stashed their vehicles and where the sensors and alarms had been, along with the patrol plans. Things may have changed, so we were taking a big risk. Without new intel of the area, we were about to approach a defended fortress.

"How are we going to get into the bunker?" I asked Linda, already knowing one way.

"The same way you got out, a place my dear daughter failed to mention she'd explored."

"That's what I figured," I told her.

We rode in silence. I didn't want to give the truck

too much gas or go so fast that the sound of the motor and wind masked any early warning signs. All of us wore radios and vests but Emily and me. We couldn't find one small enough for her, even adjusting things down. We'd have to be extra careful. With apprehension, I rolled past the farm. Part of me wanted to stop, to see if anybody had come back, if any of Lance's slaves had been left behind. I could see the progress on the fields they'd made. I couldn't tell what they'd planted, but we were getting close to winter.

"Go through town," Linda said shortly.

"Michael, you read?" Linda asked.

We all were monitoring the same frequency that Jackson, Rolston and Michael were. It was a separate one from what any of the home guard was using, with a different encryption key.

"Copy that," he said.

"Anything?"

"Nope. Couple curious people came by, told them what you wanted me to."

"You take note of who it was?"

"Sure did. They said good hunting, and they hope you take out as many of the bastards as you can."

"Sounds fantastic. The boys doing all right?" Linda asked, though I knew she was asking about the sheriff and his nephew.

"Staying out of trouble, as usual," he said with a laugh.

"Sounds good. I'll check in later. Hopefully with good news."

"You be safe Linda," he said, and everyone on the frequency could hear the tenderness in his voice.

I glanced at her, and she was turning slightly red in the face, "I will. Out."

"Copy out. I'm out. Out."

"Dork," she muttered to herself.

"He liiiiiiiiiiiiiiiiikes you," I said in a singsong voice.

"Oh, shut up," Linda snapped.

"Sorry, I know it's too soon. My sense of humor sometimes follows my foot in my mouth."

"It's..." she blew out a breath, "it's fine."

I knew it wasn't; I'd screwed up, but not on purpose. I was sure she knew that. With that though, we were in town. We rolled through slowly, barely at an idle. Everybody had their eyeballs peeled. Even Raider was looking first one direction, then another. I pet his head and he repaid my love with a lick to the side of the face. I rubbed my ear on my shoulder to hopefully wipe some of the slobber off when one of the gals behind me smacked the top of the truck.

"What do you see?" I called out of the back's open window.

23

I ROLLED to a stop at the gas station, turning the engine off. The motor ticked quietly as the metal cooled down and we all got out.

"That's what I saw," Jessica said pointing at the store.

The windows hadn't been broken like many in town that I saw, but somebody had taken the time to put newspaper over the inside of the glass. I whistled for Raider, who joined me at my side. I took my rifle out and left my door open, keys in the ignition.

"We're going to take a look," I told Jess. "You stay here and man the big gun if we need it."

"I'll cover him Jess, he's right, nobody is going to come close with that .50 ready to roll."

"How about you take over and—"

"I've got more than one reason I want you to stay back," I told her. "Please?"

"I'm not some delicate, feminine flower," she said, her lips curled into a snarl.

"No, you're not, you're a badass who could take any of us in a fair fight, and you're the best heavy machine gunner we've got. Top that off, you're carrying my baby."

She sputtered but got back in the bed of the pickup. Linda took point, with Emily and I following. We took our time, watching for movement. For some reason, the roof caught my attention. There seemed to be crows or something up there making noise. I could hear the flapping of wings.

"Hello?" Linda called out.

Nobody answered. She slung her rifle and pulled her pistol out and, using her left hand, she pushed against the door to go in. It opened, but it had been a while. Metal on metal scraped. I followed her in, my rifle at the low and ready. I was decent with my handgun, but I hadn't thought to change guns up for closer quarters. I'd have to remember that. In the day, all I used to carry was a pistol. Things had changed so much, so fast.

"Silent, 'Lil Momma and the Angry Princess are stopping to do some shopping," Jess said into the radio.

"Copy," Michael said from the homestead.

"Angry Princess?" Emily asked, bringing up the rear.

"Thirteen Ghosts," I told her, looking around the store.

It had been thoroughly looted. What food hadn't

202

been stolen had been trampled, along with the shelving that had been knocked over. An odor came from the back by the coolers. I wouldn't open those glass doors for anything.

"There's light back here," Linda said pointing to the door in the rear by the cooler that led to the small stock room.

"Raider stay by the front door," I told my pup.

Emily and I followed. The back room was full of empty boxes that had been broken down everywhere. The light came from above. There was a trap door leading to the roof, serviced by a ladder set into the wall. I was trying to hold my breath being that close to the coolers, but the ladies didn't move. I handed Linda my rifle and pulled my pistol and got up two rungs.

"What if there's fast zombies?" Linda asked suddenly.

"Double tap," I told her, then climbed up so half my body was sticking out onto the rooftop.

"Oh man," I said, looking at the dead bodies as the birds took flight.

"What is it?"

"The owner and his wife," I said, getting all the way up on the roof. "Dead."

"What happened?" Emily called.

"Fast zombies," I called back looking at them.

There was a mostly empty bottle of Jack Daniels between the bodies. The birds had been picking at them a while, but the corpses looked dried out. In the woman's hand was a bottle. I slid it out, careful not to touch her skin. Her hand had stiffened around it at one point, but as she'd dried out, her hand was left in the right shape, but I was able to extract it.

"Vicodin?" I said, looking at the nearly full to the top bottle.

There had to be more than one prescription's worth here. I shuddered at the thought, but I pocketed the pills and did a quick pat down of the bodies. Keys, wallet. No knives, no guns. They came up here to watch the stars one more time. Took a handful of pills and sipped some of Tennessee's finest before going to sleep forever. I headed back and down the ladder.

"What happened?" Emily asked quietly.

"Suicide. Booze and pills."

"Anything we can use?" Linda asked.

I holstered my pistol, fished in my pocket and pulled out the Vicodin, handing it to Linda. She whistled and twisted the cap off.

"This is the real stuff," she said, handing them back.

I pocketed them and took my rifle back. "Girl Scout, this place is a bust. Will fill you in when we head back in."

"Copy that, Silent."

We walked out slowly; I held the door for Raider. I was on edge so much that I kept expecting to hear motors fire up all around us; Keggers, zombies or some kind of looters. I looked to my dog who was just as happy and normal as normal could be. If he sensed something, he'd have been tense. Emily passed her carbine up to Jess, then jumped in the bed.

"Get in," I told Raider, pointing at my open door.

He did just as Linda was closing her door. He rewarded her with a slobbery kiss, making her laugh out loud and push him back.

"I'm sure she appreciates your concern for her skincare buddy, but I think she exfoliated about ten licks ago," I slammed my door and turned on the key.

"Emily tell her?" Linda asked.

"Yeah, she'll fill her in, or we can over the radio."

"Good, this place is creeping me out all of a sudden."

"We're not even to the compound yet," I told her.

"This is going to be a long day." Linda shuddered.

"I thought we weren't going to be starting the dance until tonight?"

"We're not, it's just that you read about what a collapse looks like, see it in other countries and try to imagine what it's like here..." her words trailed off and she looked out the window, the wind blowing her hair back.

"Fast zombies," I said softly.

"Fast zombies," she agreed.

Linda hadn't been sure of bringing Raider with us for this part, but both Jessica and I had assured her that he would listen when he needed to, and his sense of hearing and smell were far better than ours. He'd been my savior on more than one occasion now. That was how we found ourselves crawling through the brush and tall grass at the back side of the compound. We'd had to stash the truck, and Jess had disabled the .50 temporarily before we covered the truck with brush and netting.

"Patrol should be by any time now," Linda said softly into the radio.

I was under my camo netting with Raider. Jess and Emily were further up the slope than I was, and Linda had found a tree to climb and was playing long eyes for us. I shivered at that thought, the last time she'd been up high she'd sent a silenced bullet right for my brain.

One click.

This next part was my move. Jessica and I had spent two hours going over where to find the vents to the old telecom bunker that used to be hers. I waited. A mosquito tried to bite the corner of my eye and I took my hand off my gun to brush it away. When it was gone, I gripped it again. Two men were making their way warily up a well-worn path about forty feet in front of me. Both men were in their early to mid-forties if I had to guess. They wore the black tactical vests I'd come to recognize, loathe and hate with the KGR emblem on the right shoulder.

So, Henry still had them here? I wondered darkly if Spider was going to take this location over as his and dispose of Henry entirely. I grinned at that thought. If we waited long enough, would he do my light work for me?

"Targets in sight, Silent. No one walking drag that I can see."

One click.

I made sure I checked the spot where Jess and Emily had hidden. It wasn't directly in my line of sight, but I was a bit paranoid shooting uphill like this. I'd seen with my own eyes how deadly and destructive a ricochet could be.

I sighted on the first man as he pulled even with me. Both stopped, looking in my direction, their guns at the low and ready. I could feel Raider trembling in anticipation. He knew something was about to pop. I proved that right. I put the safety on PEW, then raised my shot up to the top of the man's head, using the third tick mark below the center of the scope on his face. He was close enough, but higher elevated. Straight on shot. Was he raising his gun my way?

Breathe out slowly.

The trigger broke cleanly at somewhere around five pounds. The rifle coughed. I'd already seen the bullet smack the man just above the tip of his nose as I swung the rifle an inch to the right, sighting on the second man who was turning to see what had just happened to the man falling by his side.

Breathe out slowly.

Second round fired hit him just above the ear. Both went down, twitching, their bodies not realizing they were dead already.

"Shots are good, Silent. We have a fifteen-minute window before they are missed."

"Come on boy," I said to Raider, pulling the camo netting off me and putting my gun back on safe.

I'd taken the time earlier to weave in tall grass and bits of brush to make a faux ghillie suit out of it, now I was leaving it behind and making a mad dash. I slung my rifle and held onto the butt of it, so it didn't hit me in the kidney. Raider ran beside me, giving a happy bark. I didn't scold him, I wanted him to do his usual thing. If somebody heard a bark later on, it would only help us.

My lungs burned and the contents of my backpack sloshed around, beating on my lower back. I couldn't slow down though; I'd have a five-minute window if I could do this. Brush flew by me in a blur. I had to trust Linda, Jess and Emily to be my eyes. Jess had me covered from the north, Linda from the south. My objective was to go past the cargo shaft I'd been lowered down when I'd first been shot.

I FOUND THE HATCH WHERE THE DOOR WAS AND RAN UP the hill towards the armory. I didn't go that far though, I found what Jess had told me about but had nearly missed it. Brown paint on the rocks, almost matching it. I pulled at the vines growing there and found two vents twelve inches across, the vegetation almost covering them low to the ground. When Jess had been here before, it had been her job to uncover all the vents as things grew up, which was why she'd found her way in. After we'd talked, nobody felt truly safe about going all the way in, and if they'd changed the locks or added new ones, we'd have to shoot our way in and ruin the surprise.

I was breathing hard, looking at the steep slope I was about to climb, some of it with handholds and rocks. I'd climbed harder as a kid, but there was a lot on the line. I tried to scamper up it like a cracked-out monkey but ended up being more like a meth'd-out squirrel. Adrenaline and purpose gave me a sure-foot-edness that I hadn't expected. I paused half a second to catch my breath, when Raider bounded up and then sat down next to me, his tongue hanging out.

Now for the fun. I could see the vents sticking up. They had tin caps to keep water from going down into them. I checked the first one and couldn't feel any airflow, so I moved to the one a couple feet away and felt under the cap. Bingo. Air was moving up and out. Time to make things difficult. I took my pack off and pulled out my gloves. I imagined the tin was going to be sharp, but then thought better of pulling the cap and tossed those to the side. I didn't need to take the cap off. Grinning, I started wrapping the pipe, the opening and the cap like it was shrink wrap. Small amounts of air pushed through in a couple of places, but I didn't have enough to wrap it completely airtight.

Oh well!

Next, I crawled over to the intake pipe. I couldn't

feel the air flowing in, but this was the only other option up here. Jess said these two worked as a combination of intake and exhaust for the air circulation for the lower levels. That was perfect for what I had in mind. I pulled my glove back on and started wrenching on the cap until I'd bent it enough out of the way so I could pour directly down. Raider licked my ear and I tried not to laugh. I was about to do something Jess had originally asked me not to do, but the goal here wasn't to kill those inside, but to send them running out.

I took out the two-gallon jugs of bleach and the two containers of ammonia I'd kept in the shine room to clean things and popped the caps. I held my breath and started pouring. Thirty seconds, and I was pouring the last two jugs. I turned my head and took a thin breath, then tossed those to the side and pushed down on the tin cap. I'd wrap this one too, but I was out. The fans deep below would spread the chlorine gas that was already starting to waft in my direction.

"Silent Hunter here, delivery is made. Getting into position."

"Lil Momma ready."

"Girl Scout and Angry Princess are ready for your retreat."

"Everyone in black vests are considered a target of opportunity, Silent. Keep an eye out for Henry. If you see him..." her words trailed off in my ear.

"On it," I said.

I'd crawled to the top edge. For anybody looking

straight up the cliff face that the big doors were set into, I might be visible, but I was a good fifty to seventy feet above them, and I was hoping not to shoot straight down, not yet.

"Movement at the doors," Jess said.

I would be shooting, as well as Linda Carpenter. Jess and Emily were upslope from where I'd been, and they had an angle to shoot at anybody trying to get behind me. I took magazines out of my pouch and put the two green taped ones to the left of my elbow. Using my bag as a rest, I worked on slowing my breathing and started scanning below. Normal activity? There was hardly anybody in sight. There was maybe three or four in the distance near Henry's cabin, but it would be a far shot. I really wanted the bunker confusion before I shot, so I waited more.

"Doors open, people coming out. Now running," Linda said softly.

I could see them, but the angle was wrong unless I moved closer to shoot almost straight down. That'd leave me visible, so I waited. I could hear shouts and coughs. I heard a radio below as the first group of the KGRs started boiling into my sight picture. I let a dozen get out before I started settling my crosshairs on a target.

"Engaging," Linda said softly.

"Same," I said and let my breath out slowly, adjusting my aim for shooting down sharply.

The rifle was as quiet as I remembered it. My first shot hit the man I'd been scoping out a little to the left of where I'd been aiming. The warm blood and spray the guy in front of him got made him turn as much as the body hitting him. I let the trigger reset and then slowly squeezed it again. The second shot took this one just above the vest, a low shot. Still, it did the job, he dropped. That was when all hell broke loose.

I was scanning for another target when three men in the front went down. Somebody screamed sniper and for a second, the bunched-up group started running into each other trying to find cover. I emptied my magazine with quick shots into the knot of people, not really aiming but spraying. Several more fell, but as somebody went down, he sprayed his M4 up in the air, and into the backs of those unfortunate enough to be in front of him.

"Silent Hunter, this is Michael. The chickens have left the henhouse."

"What?" I asked.

"It's time to make like a tree."

"I have sights on Henry," Linda said, "Taking the sho—"

I heard unsuppressed fire over her radio and moved my gun in her direction. Two men were about two hundred yards from Linda and were shooting into the trees. I was sure it wasn't their fire I'd heard, but they were in her ballpark. I changed my mags and let the bolt slide home and let my breath out again slowly, the adrenaline making my hands shake a bit. My first shot hit the man right in the back, my second shot missed entirely.

The man was screaming and rolling on the ground, but I couldn't hear him. I couldn't hear much. I tried to focus on the second man, but he was running and in the tree line.

"Lil Momma?"

"I'm fine," she said, her breath coming out in gasps. "Somebody happened to be close by. Never saw them."

"Did you get your shot in?" I asked.

"No. You heard Arch Angel, time to move. Girl Scout?"

"Ready to roll."

I heard a boom and a large puff of powder rolled out from their position. Then another and another.

"Time to go, boy," I told Raider, slinging my back-pack over my shoulders then grabbing my gun again.

I wanted to just run, but shots had started hitting the rock face below me as the men recovered and were testing out where the sniper fire was coming from. Nothing was near me, but I wasn't going to make their life easy.

I started crawling down the same way I'd come back up, but it was so steep I had to put my stomach against the rocks. Raider waited above for me to get out of the way.

"Hold it." The voice was almost guttural.

I turned slowly, my hands up. Two of the KGR men were standing about twenty feet from me.

"Lovely day for a hike, huh?" I asked.

"Drop it," one of them motioned to me with the point of his AK.

I slowly put my rifle down, careful not to get the suppressor in the dirt before standing back up slowly, letting my hands dangle at my sides.

"Come with us," the first man said again.

"Don't you mean both of us?" I asked them.

"Both?" the second man asked.

With my left hand I pointed up with my thumb.

Both men's eyes looked up over my shoulder as I screamed, "Támadás!"

Raider's leap was perfect, his body cross-checking both men in the chest above their guns. One of them pulled the trigger as he fell, killing the dirt at my feet. I pulled at the 1911 on my hip and the suppressor snagged. I pushed down and pulled up again as the man Raider wasn't using as a chew toy had rolled to the side, trying to bring his gun up to bear.

I fired first. The 1911 made an almost wet slapping sound as two slugs spit out, hitting him in the throat and the bottom of the chin. I ran forward, looking for a shot, but Raider had the man's gun arm and was shaking it back and forth like he was trying to break it. The man had started yelling, beating at my dog's side with his free hand. I ran closer, and without slowing, kicked him in the head. I felt the impact all the way up to my knee and tumbled over him.

Raider broke off and came over to me, licking my face. The man groaned and rolled to his stomach. I held the .45 out with one hand and fired two at him. Rorschach. I knew I'd have nightmares about this later on, but right now, I was somewhat appreciative of how quiet the gun was and how the hollow points worked from six feet away.

"You ok, boy?" I asked Raider who'd backed up when I'd shot the second man.

He whined, holding his leg up, the same one he'd been dinged in by a fragment. I holstered my .45 as I retrieved my rifle.

"You saved my butt again pup," I told him.

"Silent Hunter, this is Girl Scout. I don't see you."

"Got tripped up," I told her, "Come on Raider."

Both of us jogged with a limp back to the meeting point, my foot sore.

24

"PULL OFF HERE," Linda told me.

We'd been riding closer and closer to the compound. We could hear vehicles roaring to life down the cow path they'd called a two-track. Linda had known about this spot from living there forever. We'd put the .50 back on its mount and Jess had reloaded it, getting ready. Emily had assured me she knew how to keep linking the belts. It was easy, she said. I hoped she was right, because I wanted to hit them and run. I was out-voted, they wanted to hurt them and put more fear into them than we'd originally counted on.

The first truck was bumping down the road slowly, men standing everywhere. I could barely see them, but all along Linda's side had cedars, four big ones growing in tight together. They wouldn't make a good bullet stop, but they made a good ambush point.

"When you hear the buzz saw open up," Jess said

over the radio, "gun it. We might only get the one truck."

"Got it," I said through the open window.

She was reverting to training where everyone had headsets. We still had to push buttons, but I was guessing she'd used both so much it was just coming naturally. The truck got closer and closer. I could see the front of the hood and the windshield by the time Jess opened fire. The hood flew off as the first salvo ripped into it. I hit the gas and started moving as she raked the truck from twenty or thirty feet away. I looked in the review mirror as I saw a man in the back lob something our direction. I hit the gas hard.

"Down," I heard Jess scream.

An explosion went off behind us, and in the side mirror I could see the man's throw must have been cut short. The grenade he'd lobbed had been off course and had gone off under the still rolling truck. Men were screaming and bailing out as Jess got back up and opened up with the big gun again. I kept driving, reassured by seeing two sets of legs in the bed of the truck.

"Keep going," Jess said over the radio, her gun falling silent.

"Copy. Heading to second point?" I asked into the radio.

"Arch Angel," Linda said, "need details."

"Get back to the homestead," was all he said in reply.

"Hold on," I called loud enough for the girls in the back to hear things.

We almost rocketed onto the main road, but I didn't have time to watch the speedometer. I was trying not to throw the ladies in the back out, but there was an urgency in Michael's voice I didn't like.

"What do you think happened?" I asked Linda.

"He didn't say, and there's only a few of us on the channel," Linda said. "I haven't heard from Jackson and Rolston in a while."

"Should we pull them up on the radio?" I asked her.

"No... Arch Angel, what are scouts reporting?" Linda asked.

"Busy," was his terse reply.

I DIDN'T SLOW DOWN MORE THAN NECESSARY. A SENSE OF urgency had overtaken me. If Michael had things to report to us, he would have. I had to trust in him. I know Linda did. We shot through town, breaking the 25mph speed limit by a lot, and I only slowed to take the turn to the most direct route to the homestead.

"Change frequencies," I told Linda. "I want to see what we're driving back into."

"Already did," Linda said, her face grim. "Several scout outposts not responding on the western edge again, including the one from before."

"Dammit," I cursed.

Raider whined at hearing my anger and pushed his snout into my side, rubbing his head against my right arm. I downshifted through the turn, and then scratched his head as I sped back up and shifted again. His body went stiff as he made another sound. I saw he was looking intently past me, to the left. I spared a glance out the window when the silence was shattered by gunfire. I swerved, sending the rear end onto the gravel side of the dirt road. I fought the wheel, but smoke or steam had erupted from the hood and I was losing speed fast.

Linda was screaming into her radio, her words lost to me as the .50 opened up from behind me in a long stream of smoke, fire and death. Something exploded on the side of the road behind us.

"Can we make it back?" Emily shouted as something in the engine compartment started banging.

"I think so," I told her, "if there aren't any more surprises."

The big gun went quiet again.

"You ok, Girl Scout?" I asked over the radio.

"Yeah, but all this fun has me feeling like I'm on the world's worst roller coaster," she said simply, "and I have to pee."

"Raider, you ok?" I asked, feeling the adrenaline dump that had hit my bloodstream start to wear off.

Raider chuffed and licked my face as I crested the last hill to the homestead. Smoke was billowing from the back of the barn, and people with buckets were running everywhere. The garden hose was stretched to fill buckets and several people were taking turns at the hand pump. The truck let out a large bang and the engine died. I fought the wheel and brakes. With no power assist, it took all my strength to slow the truck down enough to turn into our drive. I struggled to turn right after my left turn and started rolling into the grass near the house, almost standing on the brakes.

I reached down and pulled the emergency brake when we'd almost come to a stop. Linda was out of the truck, grabbing her rifle in a flash. Raider followed her out her side as more smoke billowed from the hood. Now that I'd stopped, it was blinding, thick. I smelled burning oil. I got out as fast as I could and when my right foot hit the ground, I fell. Blinding pain came out of the ankle of the foot I'd kicked the man in the head with. I was rolling over to push myself up when somebody grabbed me by the belt and hauled me up and backward.

Emily.

"There's some kind of fire, are you ok?" she asked me.

"Ankle. Must have banged it up," I said between gasps, using the side of the truck to hold myself up.

"Wes!" Jess called.

She'd pulled the pin holding the .50 mount and was lifting the big gun. "Here, I can't do more than lift it."

"Take my bag and gun," I told Emily, "I don't know if the truck is going to go up!"

"You can't walk on that ankle," Emily shouted at me as she was taking my things.

"Improvise. We can't lose the gun—"

"I'll help him," Jess screamed, her arms straining as she lifted the big gun straight up and over to me.

Half a belt was still in the gun, and I hoisted it over my left shoulder, holding onto the barrel before letting go with my right hand and testing my foot. Agony shot up, but I didn't wobble. Jess reached down and put an ammo can on the side of the bed and hopped off.

"What about the other one?" I asked as she picked it up and got on my right side.

"Used it up," she said, "Let's go. It might not snuff itself out,"

I started walking slowly, but the pain was horrible. Jess saw that and switched the can to her right hand and got her left shoulder under my right one. I reached down and grabbed her belt and together we crab-walked to the porch where I set the big gun down. The sucker felt like it weighed all of a hundred pounds or more. Emily was sitting there, guns and packs discarded. She was holding Mary tight to her chest, rocking her. I staggered to the porch and pulled Emily's arm back.

Mary was sobbing, but I couldn't hear over the shouts. She had blisters up the side of her neck and over part of her face in a thin line, and the edges of her hair were singed and burnt. I sat down hard and pried her from Emily's arms. She resisted for a moment, then let me take the child. Mary batted my hands away when I touched near her neck. I was going to pull the collar of her shirt back to see how far the burns went but could see now that it didn't. I grabbed her arms, holding her hands out so I could inspect them one after another. Her right hand was blistered on the palm, but other than that, I couldn't see anything else.

"She's burned, but she's going to be ok," I told Emily, handing the girl back to her.

She buried her unburned skin against her mom's neck, sobbing.

Jess was pulling at me, screaming we had to go. I shot a glance back at the truck and saw the smoke had relented some, but wisps of it coming out from under the hood still. Jess pulled on my shoulder and I awkwardly got to my feet again. Jess put her shoulder under my arm again and I let her help me to the hand pump where a red-faced Curt was working the handle.

"Where's Margie?" I asked him, concerned that I didn't see her with him.

"Hauling buckets," he said, gasping for breath.

"Where'd my mom go?" Jessica asked him.

I was shaking my foot, trying to loosen it up some. The pain was there, but it wasn't as crippling as it had been before. I pulled myself from Jess and stood on it experimentally.

"Communications," Curt said, finishing filling a bucket while a sweaty-faced teen boy was waiting.

Another bucket was put down and Curt started pumping, the plump man sweating.

"Let me spell you for a bit," I told him, working my way behind him.

"Wes, you can't walk," Jessica yelled.

"It's not as bad as it was," I told her. "Go find your

mom and figure out what's going on. I'm not going to let Curt stroke out here."

Jess nodded, then left for the barn. Where the hell was my dog?

"Raider?" I called as Curt moved aside to let me get behind the long arm.

I started pumping, scanning for my dog. Above the screams I heard barking, then Raider ran from behind the house with something in his mouth.

"What happened?" I asked Curt, wincing as I pumped, the ankle not as bad as I'd originally feared. I hoped.

"A fire broke out at the back of the barn. Don't know why. We immediately dumped all the water on it we could, and we've got all available water sources draining to fight it. Some of ours were hurt getting out. Mary was back there with the other kids—"

"Did we lose anyone?" I asked.

"We got all the kids out. We'll have to take a headcount when this is done. I don't think we'll lose the barn, but whatever started that fire didn't go right out with water. We're wetting everything around it but had to pull sections of barn wood off it. Then the kid manning this started puking so I jumped on this."

I felt like puking. Raider had stopped at my feet and dropped a plump rabbit, his tail wagging. "Good boy," I told him. "Go find Grandma."

He barked and took off running. I was starting to get winded myself when Sheriff Jackson came running up with a bucket. He took one look at me and shook his head.

"What happened, Sheriff?" I asked him.

"This wasn't an accidental fire and I can't find my nephew," he said, talking softly, though the line of kids and adults with buckets was moving through quickly now. "You need me to take a turn?"

"Yeah, I'm..." I started sliding sideways, but Curt grabbed my arm in a vice-like grip.

"I've got you; don't you go passing out on me, boy!"

"I'm not, I ... sprained ankle. Pain snuck up on me," I said through gritted teeth.

Jessica came running out of the barn, coughing. Her hat had come off at some point, and her hair was flowing behind her as her gun beat against her side.

"Mom?" I asked her.

"She's on the radio, she's fine. You're needed inside there," she said, pulling me back. "Sorry Sheriff."

"I got this ma'am," Sheriff Jackson said, taking my place and pumping.

25

"GOOD EVENING WESTLEY. What a good time for a bonfire, wouldn't you agree?" Spider's voice came out of the base station, and I saw it was on the frequency we'd used before when we'd wanted to talk privately.

"It is." I coughed. "What do you want?"

"I will say, I was surprised you got away so easily from Henry's teams. They've grown lax. Mine, however, have not. You really thought you could hit us without some kind of response? The moment you left; we started the fires."

My blood ran cold at that. Not only did he have someone inside here, but he had people close enough to set some sort of incendiary. Something I'd have to think about for a bit, because I was pretty sure the fire that couldn't be put out was thermite.

"I don't know, every time we've gone up against your boys, we keep stacking the corpses like cordwood. How many did you lose this time? Ten? Fifteen?"

"How many did you lose?" Spider asked, a hint of amusement in his voice.

"Nobody was seriously hurt in the fires, so what's the point?" I asked him.

"I didn't ask how many were hurt and killed, I asked you how many did you lose?"

"Why are you calling me?" I asked him, avoiding the question, and fearing the answer.

"To tell you that not only do I have teams close, close enough to light fires right on your doorstep, but that my men are good enough to snatch yours, which is what I've done. Yes, you bloodied my nose a little bit at the survivalist compound, but most of those were conscripts. You've hardly faced any real soldiers."

"My intel tells me that most of your soldiers were dishonorable discharges, a lot of them weren't even gunners."

"True, but a lot of them are. At least as many of them as your entire compound. Plus, I've got specialists. Men who've done snatch and grabs, arson and unconventional warfare that makes what the VC did look like child's play by comparison. I've already told you as much, and you've got a traitor close to you, yet you still won't give yourself up. It's just a matter of time. If you don't come yourself, I'll have you snagged as well."

"What I don't understand, is if you have so many people who are that good, why haven't you snagged me and Marshall already?" I asked him, finding a hole in his logic.

"Because I was asked nicely by a friend not to injure you any more than is necessary for your capture."

"A friend?" I asked him, surprised. Who would ask a favor of this self-proclaimed warlord, king to be?

"Yes, you see, even evil men such as myself have friends, and unless one such as I don't listen to the requests friends, they will hardly be in a position to return the favor someday. Don't you see?"

"So, you can't snag me, because I'm too much of a hard target, and you're worried that it'd have killed me otherwise."

"Certain of it," Spider admitted. "The reasonable thing would be for you to walk out to the end of the driveway and let my team bring you back in."

"Where are the scouts?" I asked the small group around me.

"None of them have reported in," Michael said, his face drawn and pale.

"If he took out all twelve positions..." Linda mused.

"Should we break up into small groups and go into hiding?" Jessica asked her mom, who was already shaking her head no.

"If you've got men across the street, why not come get me yourself?" I asked him.

"Because you're in the barn right now, and around a big group of people. If I dropped a mortar to take out your cadre of do-gooders, I might take you out by mistake, and I did promise..."

"You want me, come and get me," I snarled.

"It might come to that. Soon, Westley Flagg, soon. If you don't hand yourself over tonight, you can expect to be putting out a lot of fires in the coming days. Too bad about the barn, I was hoping it'd burn down."

"Your thermite didn't do the trick," I told him softly.

"Figured it out, did you? Good. I always heard you were a smart boy."

"I thought you didn't know who I was at first?" I asked him, confused.

"Oh, I didn't. I didn't realize who you were when you first attacked. But it's come to my attention that somebody in a position to know you rather well has mentioned you to me before. I find the phrase 'it's a small world', rather inadequate, don't you?"

"He's messing with your head again," Jessica said, putting her arms around my back, hugging me.

"I know, it's just that..." I broke off.

He was hitting close to home. It was like he really did have an inside person. He knew of me, had heard about me? This was confusing.

"Westley?" Grandma's voice called from the barn doorway, waving her hand to clear the air.

"Over here!" I called, happy to see her and Raider.

"Your fool dog won't quit pulling me," she said, rubbing her arm.

"Sorry, I couldn't find you and he's not limping as bad as me," I told her.

"Things getting busy there Wes?" Spider asked over the radio.

Grandma walked closer as I turned to the radio. "I don't understand how an evil bastard like you can sleep at night."

"Easy, I put my head on the pillow. How can a selfish bastard like you sleep at night knowing all this pain, suffering and bloodshed could end by giving yourself up?"

"Eat shit," I said into the mic and stood up, wrapping my arms around Grandma.

She hugged me back hard. "Poor Mary, that little girl..."

"What's wrong?" I asked her, I'd seen the burn marks, but it hadn't seen anything super serious.

"Her poor face," Grandma said.

"I know, she's got a line of blisters," I said, drawing a line up my neck and cheek with a finger. "She's going to be ok, Grandma."

"Emily won't be. I need you. I was trying to calm her down but she's..."

"I'll go with you," Jessica said, pulling on me.

"Looks like I'll see you sooner or later," Spider's voice came out of the small speaker.

I gave the radio my middle finger in a gesture of maturity.

JESSICA HELD ONTO THE BACK OF MY BELT, THOUGH I WAS a lot steadier on my feet than I had been earlier. I had my right arm over her shoulder, with Grandma and

Raider on my right. Yaeger and Diesel were following close behind. They'd been lying near the hand pump when we'd come out of the barn, the bigger dog pulling the rabbit Raider had caught into smaller pieces and eating it. I shuddered but kept going. Jessica growled low in her throat herself at seeing that but kept going. Before we got to the porch, I could hear Emily's screams.

Jessica let me go as soon as we reached the railing. She rushed ahead, and into the house. Grandma went in as well. I worked my way up slowly, hearing Jessica start screaming at her to calm down, she was scaring her daughter. I pushed the door open and saw both ladies standing almost nose to nose shouting at the top of their lungs. Mary was sitting on the couch, pressed so far back into it that it looked like she was trying to hide. She had the throw blanket covering her, but I saw one of the washcloths pressed against the side of her face. She was crying, but this time I could clearly see fear written across her face.

"Stop it!" I yelled, projecting my voice as loud and as hard as I could.

For a moment there was silence, then sobbing. I hobbled to the middle of the living room where Jessica and Emily were standing. Both were crying harder now, shaking. Grandma sat down on the couch next to Mary, her hand smoothing the little girl's hair out.

"I can't... It's too much, I can't keep my daughter safe. It's somebody's—"

I'd seen her wind up and swing a chair at me

before, and she had that look now. Her body tensed, and I could tell it was Jessica she was focused on. I moved quickly just as she was balling a fist. I stepped in behind her and wrapped both arms around her, pinning her arms at her sides, and picked her up. She went wild. I took a shot to the chin from the top of her head, her nails digging into my jeans, trying to scratch me, while a string of curses spewed from her mouth. She turned, trying to bite at me as I pulled her backward to the end of the couch and sat down. I wrapped first one leg, then another over her and squeezed. A breath went out of her, then I felt her breath hitching as she struggled to breathe back in. I let the pressure up some and held her there.

IT TOOK US TWENTY MINUTES OF ME HOLDING HER STILL like that for her to break. She started wheezing softly, her body going limp. My arms were bloody from her nails, my face and chest sore from the repeated headbutts. Grandma had taken Mary back into her and Grandpa's bedroom, so she didn't see her mother lose her mind completely. I was scared, this woman was a loose cannon and she'd come completely unhinged.

"I'm getting Mom in here to look at you," Jessica said after a moment. "If we need to, we can tie her up to one of the wooden chairs."

"I ... why are you ... don't tie me up, I need my daughter."

"Look what you did to Wes!" Jessica said angrily.

Emily sniffed and then looked straight down at her lap. "Is my daughter ok?" she asked in a quiet voice, sniffing.

"Yes," I told her. "Grandma took her in the back room while you had your meltdown."

"You think I'm crazy, don't you?" she asked me quietly.

"You completely came unhinged right there," I told her. "I don't know what to think."

"I'm... sorry ... your poor arms."

I let her go. Jess watched her warily. In the fracas, Jess had put down her rifle somewhere, but her hand rested on her pistol. Her meaning was clear. Emily got up off my lap and started for the hallway.

"Wait," I called to her, "let Grandma bring her out. You terrified Mary."

"I..." whatever she was going to say was forgotten as she went to the sink.

She turned on the water, the pressure low, and started washing my blood off of her hands, her motions frantic.

"Lil Momma, Girl Scout here."

"Read you Girl Scout," I heard out of my radio. I'd forgotten the earbud was still in.

"I need you to bring one of those good medical packs to the house."

"How bad?"

"Might need the morphine; bad."

"Copy that."

I looked at my arms. They hurt, they had bled quite a bit, but the pain wasn't all-consuming.

"I'm sorry, I didn't mean to hurt you so bad," Emily said again.

"The morphine isn't for him," Jessica told her. "It's to knock your ass out if you snap again."

Emily turned to her in shock.

"You've been a loose cannon for a while now," I reminded her. "Remember in the bunker when Mary needed a transfusion? You lost it and took a folding chair to me."

Jessica was the one doing a double take at that.

"And until you calmed down, it was all I could do to avoid the blows. My only other option was to hurt you. You were losing control today the same way. This time though, you did it in front of your daughter."

Emily's chest heaved, and she started sobbing again. She turned the water off and sat down on the floor in front of the sink, pulling her knees up to her chin, head down. Linda rushed in a second later, and from the back I heard Raider bark. Good, he'd gone in with Grandma. He'd comfort her and keep her safe. Then I looked around, where were the other two dogs?

"How bad—" Linda saw Emily on the floor sobbing and me getting up slowly.

She motioned for me to come forward and I did.

"Right ankle at least sprained," Jessica said, "but mostly scratches on his arms."

"Morphine?" Linda asked as Emily cried louder.

Jessica sat down two chairs away and pulled my

right leg up and set it on the chair between us. I put my arms on the table, thankful Grandma had her plastic tablecloth on it. I could wash it up easily. Linda looked at me, puzzled, and I nodded at Emily. Linda rolled her eyes and opened the case that had the syringes. She showed me the bottle she had when we'd been interrogating the man at the roadside, her eyebrow raised.

It was the sedative. I nodded. She got a needle out, took the top off and pulled the plunger up. Then she pulled the needle out of the bottle, raised it up and pushed the air out. I held my hand out, and she hesitated. Emily was looking at us, her body trembling.

"Morphine?" she asked me.

"No, I forgot we had this," I told her. "This is a sedative. I'm guessing this is enough to make you sleep for a while. Half this should get you calm, am I right?" I asked Linda.

Linda hesitated again, then nodded and handed me the needle.

"I don't want to sleep; I need to check on Mary." Her voice was small, almost childlike.

"How about a compromise?" I asked her, "we'll give you half and see if you can stay calm enough."

"Only ... only if you do it," she said, nodding at the needle in my hand.

Jessica started working on my boot, undoing my laces. She nodded at me in agreement. Linda tossed a package of alcohol swabs to me that had been torn open on one side.

"Come up here," I told Emily, patting my legs.

She was so short I couldn't reach her from the floor near me.

She got to her feet slowly, her arms around her middle section hugging herself, and walked over. She looked at Jess, who nodded her head at me. Slowly, Emily sat on the edge of my lap. I pulled the swabs with my left hand and cleaned a spot on her right shoulder. My boot came off, making my leg spasm in pain. Emily jerked, but I took a deep breath and put my left arm around her already bloody middle from scratching me up earlier, to hold her steady. I took her right arm with my left hand.

"Please don't move," I told her.

"I trust you," Emily said quietly through the tears.

It was hard at this angle, but I got the needle into the ball of muscle in her shoulder and depressed it until half the liquid was gone. I pulled it out as she shuddered and held it out to my side. Linda took it, putting a cap on it.

"How long does it take?" Emily asked.

Linda was holding up her hands now

Ten fingers. She breathed.

Nine fingers. Emily tensed, her breath hitching, calming.

Eight fingers. She breathed out heavily.

Seven fingers. She sniffed, taking a deep breath.

Six fingers. She leaned her back against my chest.

Five fingers. I could feel her body relax slightly.

Four fingers. Her head rolled back, resting on my collar bone.

Three fingers. I had to hold her tighter, she was almost sliding off my lap.

Two fingers.

"Wes, if something happens to me, take care of my baby. Please."

One finger. Her body went completely still.

Her eyes were still open, her breathing normal, but a little slower. I was worried we had given her enough to knock her out, but she spoke again.

"Promise me," she whispered.

"I promise," I told her.

"I don't know if I'm cut out for this world anymore," she said softly.

I wiped my eyes with my free hand and saw similar reactions from the others. Grit had gotten into their eyes at some point too.

"Here, I'll help you go to the couch," Linda said, "then I'm going to fix up Wes."

"Just take care of him. I'll be ok—"

"Come on sweetie," Linda said softly, taking the smaller woman under the arms, helping her stand, then walking her to the couch.

Jessica touched my hand. I saw she was crying again too. I put my hands in hers and squeezed once. She squeezed back.

26

ONE TEAM of our roving scouts were all dead. Twelve of our lookout points had had their entire teams killed. We had twelve people unaccounted for, including Luke, the man I'd found in the woods. Elias, the one who'd turned traitor, and then flipped again, was also gone ... and Deputy Rolston. Nobody had seen or heard a thing. The fire had been set, probably after all the lookouts and scouts had been taken out, our people snatched and not one single shot fired. Confusion, fear and my failure to prevent something like this from happening was weighing heavily on me. Spider hadn't been joking when he said his men were good.

WHO HAD WE BEEN KILLING?

.   .   .

Digging the graves took too damned long. There weren't enough people to man the lookout points and do the work that needed to be done. That was how I found myself out there as an extra set of eyes. My ankle was sore as all get out, but the swelling hadn't been as bad as I'd thought it might have been. I must have hurt it when kicking that man's head like a football, but the adrenaline had masked the pain at the time.

Three days later it wasn't as horrible, and I was able to get around with the aid of Grandpa's cane and half doses of the Vicodin. I could stand in one spot without it but moving hurt. I'd taken to leaving my long gun on the porch but wore my suppressed .45 everywhere now. I was with Jessica as her and Emily took turns digging. The homestead was split between numbed terror and an anger so deep that shouting matches had erupted almost hourly in the barn.

Emily had sat on the couch for the most of that day, staring off into space and wiping her nose with tissues that Grandma provided. Mary had come out of Grandma's room that night and sat on the couch near Emily, but she wasn't snuggled in. Raider was going to get that spot, but Yaeger beat him to it and pressed his body and chest against her, forcing her to wrap an arm around him before he laid across her lap.

I'd heard Jessica whisper a command to him. He wasn't just providing comfort; he was keeping her right there. Sadly, I had agreed at the time, but now, days later... I felt horrible for the things I'd said to Emily. It was obvious to us that she'd had mental issues before, but with what she'd gone through, we'd made allowances for that. She'd completely snapped the night her daughter had gotten burned. Mary had been hurt, but not horribly, and the piece of burning wood that had popped and hit her hadn't done as much damage as first thought. Her burns were already drying out and scabbing up.

Grandma had been using an aloe mixture on her burns and had almost stripped her entire plant to provide enough for everyone who'd gotten burned fighting the fire. Right now, though, Emily was doing her job stoically. She'd stripped to a sports bra and jeans, sweat beading on her body. I felt bad letting her do the work, but I couldn't step on a shovel just yet.

"You two don't have to watch me," Emily said finally, turning to face us, a smear of earth across one cheek where she'd wiped her gloved hands.

"I'm not here to watch you," I told her quietly.

"You sure are getting an eyeful if you're not," she snapped back, a hint of a smile tugging at the side of her mouth.

"I—"

"She got you there," Jessica said, then giggled.

WTH?

"I'm sorry I can't do more. I'm here for moral support," I said quietly.

"You're sure you're not here to restrain me if I go off the deep end again?" she asked, "you know, make me sit on your lap a couple of more times?" She waggled her eyebrows.

"Oh my, she's definitely back to normal." Jessica giggled as my face burned.

"What's so funny?" I asked, turning to my fiancé.

"She's doing it to make you turn beet red, and it always works. Every single time!"

Emily nodded and faked a curtsey, then turned back to work.

"Besides," I said, "this is lonely work and you can always use an extra set of eyes this close to the road."

"I know. Thank you," she said softly, "you both have put up with me... I know part of me is broken," she said still shoveling, "but you're not treating me like some sort of freak."

"You're not a freak," I told her, "and I'm sorry for being so harsh the other day."

"Although your bedside manner sucks, Dr. Flagg, the message was true." She kept shoveling. "What do you think, deep enough?"

"Let me hop in for a few more," Jessica said.

Emily took off her gloves and handed them plus the shovel to Jessica, who hopped in the grave. I looked; there were too many freshly dug graves from this past summer. We'd lost so many, men and women, some I'd never even learned their names. We'd had people coming in from time to time but that had stopped. I had an idea where the rest of them had gone, or rather, been taken.

Spider's labor pool, or should I say slaves, were working the farm fields and other projects at that evil bastard's whim. In a way, it was work that needed to be done and it would help the overall long-term survival of people, but at what cost? Was having food good enough of a reason to remain a slave? While talking to Luke before he was taken, he'd told me that life as one of Spider's slaves hadn't been easy, and for the women and children it was downright barbaric. I didn't doubt him. He seemed to have all the supplies he needed, yet he was farming and bartering people off for what?

"Thanks, I could sit a spell," Emily said, plopping in the grass next to me.

"How's Mary today?" I asked her.

"You know, she's asking about you. Hopes now that we're living in the barn that you won't forget about her."

"I won't forget about her," I told her. "I love that kid to pieces."

Emily looked at me hard and then nodded. "Please don't forget your promise. If something happens to me..."

"It won't," I said, trying not to choke up with the fast-paced change of her mood and the subject matter, "besides, I seem to be a shit magnet. I think something is more likely to happen to me before it'll happen to you." I pointed at my ankle, which was wrapped tight.

"You do seem to get dinged up quite a bit," she mused, "but you have this uncanny way of..."

"He keeps going, he's still surviving," Jessica finished off for her.

"That's it," Emily said snapping her fingers. "He's a survivor. So, Wes, don't ever give in to Spider. We'll figure something out. You don't have to give yourself up."

"Don't be so flippant about that," I told her, "he wants you ladies too. Probably to hurt me, but he made that clear."

"That scares me," Jessica said, her back turned, still digging.

"That looks good," Curt said, walking up behind us.

We all turned to see him and the sheriff carrying a body that had been wrapped in sheets somebody had found somewhere, the cloth tied around the body.

"Where's his family?" I asked, looking at the wrapped package.

"You dug that grave earlier," Curt said nodding to the filled-in hole to the left, "and this one is a her. Part of our scout teams."

I looked down and said a silent prayer. Jessica got out of the hole, tossing the shovel and gloves off to the side.

"Curt, let me get your end, you look beat," Jessica told him.

"I've got one more left in me, might do some digging later on too."

Curt wouldn't be doing any digging; he was red in

the face and still seriously out of shape. It might kill him.

We watched as the silent sheriff and Curt lowered the body into the ground as gently as possible. Curt gave us a small wave, huffing for breath, walking in the direction of the water pump. Sheriff Jackson picked up the dropped shovel and started filling in the hole. Another life extinguished too early; another body buried as deep as we could. I sighed.

"We'll figure something out, Westley," Jackson said.

"I know. I ... I'm sorry about your nephew," I told him.

"I'm not one hundred percent sure he didn't realize what was going on and let himself be snatched," he said, looking around to make sure nobody else was near. There wasn't anyone. "Remember what we'd been talking about around the radio that day?"

"Yeah, but there was no solid plan, just us talking," I told him.

"Maybe he saw a good opportunity," Emily said quietly, "maybe that's what we all need. An opportunity."

"How about you three mosey up to the house and get washed up. The Marshall kid shot a wild hog earlier today. Probably taste like piss, as it was an uncut male, but I figure nobody will mind when it all comes down to it."

"What?" I asked him, my mouth suddenly going dry with the thought of ham, bacon ... something.

"Linda was teaching him how to shoot. He was

using her rifle. This big black boar walked out of the weeds with a small sounder. Probably searching for food or a place to root around."

"But we don't have ... I mean, I've never seen any around here!" The smoker and snares I'd done because it made sense, but I'd never expected them to amount to much.

"I've been sheriff of this county for going on fifteen years, was a deputy for at least that long," he tipped his hat back, wiping the sweat off his brow, "and I can't tell you how many hogs there are, but I can tell you how many pig versus car accidents we have had called in to us."

"A lot?" I asked.

"More than you'd think. Besides, there's another reason I figured you ought to clean up some."

"Yeah, why's that?" Jessica asked.

"Westley is probably the only one who knows how to butcher something like that. Him and maybe Lester. We lost a lot of good men and women. Too damned many."

Sheriff William Jackson's words were full of sorrow, but my mouth was watering. I'd never cleaned a wild boar, but I'd read about it, and worst comes to worst, I could just skin it. I remembered something about scalding them first so the hair could be scraped off, then dipping it again in boiling water to skin it. I wasn't for sure, and we didn't have any of the fancy curing salts, but now we could smoke things. Still, people had subsisted on wild game forever, and meat was meat.

"Ok, thanks for letting me know."

I started getting to my feet, but both Jessica and Emily got under my shoulders and bodily hauled me to my feet, Jessica handing me the cane.

"You know what ladies? I've been shot up, dinged up, had my skull cracked, sprained my ankle, and you've both been there to help take care of me. I appreciate that." It was the truth, but I realized that without the both of them, things would have turned out a lot different, in a lot of matters.

"That's what family is for," Emily said, giving me a quick hug, before stepping back. "Let's go, I'm dying to have some bacon. What part of the pig does bacon come from?" she asked.

"The butthole," Jessica said straight-faced.

Emily's eyes got big, then she laughed, and play pushed Jessica. The move surprised Jessica and it almost sent her to her butt. Jessica made an exasperated sound and pushed Emily back playfully. Emily pinwheeled her arms and went on her butt in an exaggerated move and rolled to her feet, a handful of sod in her hands. Her aim was perfect, and the dirt clod hit Jessica in the chest. Jessica swore and both ladies took off running, screaming, laughing, and full of shenanigans.

"You know," Sheriff Jackson said, watching them playing like they were kids, "It's moments like that, that remind me what it is we're fighting for. It's the simple things in life that I find that I've missed the most."

"Same here," I said grinning as the taller and

longer legged Jessica caught up with Emily and wrapped her arms around the smaller woman's middle and wrestled her to the ground. "Any bets on if she makes Emily eat dirt?"

"No bet," Sheriff Jackson said, turning back to the hole.

27

THE WILD BOAR had a gamy taste to it. I'd cut chunks of meat from its carcass to cook over the fire tonight. We'd saved back one of the hams and both belly sides to experiment smoking on. The rest of the pig, including some of the organ meat, was being cooked up. Almost the entire group had turned out for it. Marshall was retelling the story of shooting the big boar hog for the fourth or fifth time. Emily sat nearby, watching him intently.

I knew the boy liked her, and I had always thought Emily showed ... how do I say it? conflicted or mixed signals? It hadn't been the first time I'd noticed her interest in the younger man. Part of me wished she would make a move one way or another. I was flattered she liked me, but after a lot of thought and soul searching, that was all it was to me. She was attractive and had a wild and savage streak I found appealing in a certain way. My heart told me no, and I'd already given that up to Jess a long time ago.

"So, then I saw the branches moving and Linda and I both heard the grunting, and it stepped out. I held the rifle up the way she showed me and then pulled the trigger. I forgot to take off the safety, so by the time I got it off it had turned. I waited for my shot, then took it. He dropped right there."

I'd provided venison on a few joyous occasions to the group, but the cooking pork was making Marshall a hero here. I was glad seeing him working on ignoring the discomfort and being the center of attention. It was like he was growing up, a little bit every day. Part of me wondered if it was because he suddenly found himself in a situation where he had little to no privacy and was forced to interact more. He loved working with the little kids, and his 'class' was wildly popular with the kids. He was teaching them to read and working with the older kids on expanding their reading so Carla could handle the other things like writing and arithmetic.

"How long you got there?" Jessica asked.

I heard her stomach growl.

"Probably a few more minutes for this batch," I told her, turning the spit.

"You know, when things were normal, I'd trim all the fat off pork. It wasn't healthy. Now? I look at those chunks and I can't help but shiver knowing how nourishing it is."

"You sure you're not having random cravings again?"

"Oh, no way," Jessica told me.

Raider yawned. He'd been sitting next to me. He rolled over on his side, pressing his back against my legs. We'd found some log rounds and had been using them as a makeshift stools while we cooked. I wasn't the only one cooking either! Spits and skewers criss-crossed the big fire. The hog hadn't been a monster, but he was easily hundreds of pounds. Sheriff Jackson was supervising getting the smoker going that they'd put together before Rolston was snatched.

It was a pretty cool affair. A trench had been dug into the hillside, and some old aluminum venting had been run from the hole cut in the floor of the trailer to where the fire was going to be. Then most of the trench was backfilled with the leftover dirt, making circular walls around the area where the fire was laid and was being lit right now. The cattle panels had been cut and fit into the trailer. I'd heard that the hams were too heavy and had made the panels sag until they fell, so they'd cut large hunks of ham and hung it off the panel with chunks of twine, wire and anything else they could. It was a lot of meat, but it really wasn't. Even with our reduced numbers, the hog would be gone faster than we could smoke it. I wondered if Colton, Marshall, Brandon and Anthony had been religious about checking the snares.

"And then, Linda told me to gut it"—Marshall said, and there were a few titters from the female persuasion in the crowd— "and I was thinking, I dissected a fetal pig in eighth grade. How hard could this be? I was wrong."

Roars of laughter.

"Big hunter, come, eat," I said, pulling the spit off.

"You better not give him all of that," Jess said, her nails digging into my side.

"Easy hulk," I said, laying the spit between my knees, "I'll get you a Snickers."

Marshall walked over, and I noticed more than a couple of ladies watched him with what I could only call interest. Emily was smiling his way as well. I pulled my knife out and cut through the nearly two-inch-thick piece of meat, splitting portions into half. I used my knife to poke into it and slid it off the skewer, handing it to Jess, then the skewer to Marshall.

"I ... thank you," he said. "This is kind of weird. It's weird, right?" he asked suddenly.

"What? People appreciating what you're doing, how you're contributing, and letting you soak up the sunshine?" Jess asked him, putting the chunk of meat on one of the plates I'd brought out from Grandma's cupboards.

"Well, sort of. I mean, I just shot the thing." He looked uncomfortable, but took a bite, right off the skewer.

"A lot of folks here are afraid to leave the area around the barn and gardens," I told him, "so not only does what you did look brave in their eyes, they're now eating their first portions of pork in a long, long while."

"And don't be surprised if some of those ladies come talk to you later," Jessica said around a mouthful of hot pork.

"Why would they want to talk to me?" Marshall asked innocently.

"Maybe for a tickle fight?" I asked, trying to match his innocent tone.

It was a good thing Jessica had just swallowed her food, because she burst into giggles. I grabbed her plate before she rolled off the log round and onto the floor, holding her stomach. I started laughing as well. People looked at us, smiling, but in confusion. Yaeger and Diesel wandered into the firelight to watch as their human tried to get to her feet, dusting off her backside and taking the plate back from me. I retrieved my knife that had been dropped in the dirt and wiped it off on my pant leg and put it back in the sheath.

"Wait, you mean... Wes... I... Do you have a hat I could borrow?"

"Jessica," Emily called, "you shouldn't be rolling around on the ground like that."

"Yeah, what's this about a tickle fight?" Linda asked, joining the two pups.

Jessica started braying with laughter all over again. Raider rolled onto his stomach, then stood, pushing his nose under my arm. I patted him, stroking his fur as I decided to let Jessica or Marshall explain it to the ladies.

"I mean, I don't really have a hat, and if I'm going to try to do this right...?"

"Stop, please, stop!" Jessica was holding her stomach, "Don't make me laugh so hard."

"What's he talking about?" Linda asked me.

"You'll have to ask Jessica or Emily." I tried not to smirk as I said it.

Linda rolled her eyes. "Any more of that left?" She eyeballed Jessica's plate.

"Sure, I'll cook some up," I told her, reaching for another sharpened stick.

"You know," Linda said, plopping down just behind Jessica and me, "I'm still ... having a hard time with things. Losing Dave, my baby getting hurt... What I almost did to you—"

"I'm sorry, it's—" I started to interrupt but she put her hand over my mouth to silence me.

"But days like this, times like these, I wish it had never happened. But if Dave was here, he'd be happy. He'd be happy for Jessica and you. He liked you, Westley, and he'd have approved of you two getting hitched."

"I appreciate that," I told her.

We watched as a lady a little older than me walked up to a bemused Marshall, who was still trying to puzzle out what was funny and whispered in his ear. She pulled on his arm gently. He whispered something back, obviously a question by the puzzled look on her face. She whispered something else, a big grin lighting up her face, and hooked her arm in his.

"Here," Marshall said handing me back the half-eaten skewer of meat. "I think I'm going to go for a walk?"

"Have fun," I told him, grinning.

I pulled the chunk of meat off and offered it to Raider. He didn't quite wolf it down, but it was a near thing.

"What was that about?" Linda asked.

"Tickle fights," Jessica said, and she was off again.

I had to smile. Right now, life was good. Marshall threw me a wave over his shoulder as he and the woman walked out of the firelight, towards the back of the property. He might be innocent, but he didn't have to be a saint.

28

"SILENT HUNTER, COME IN," I heard over the radio's earpiece I'd been wearing.

"I copy you, Lil Momma," I replied.

"I've got the evil one on the horn for you," she said softly, though I could hear a din of voices in the background.

"I don't want to talk to him," I told her.

"I know, I told him as much... But he's having a moment, and you may want to come in here and listen to this."

"Copy that," I told her and then clapped Marshall on the shoulder.

We'd been checking snares. Two of them had been tripped but there wasn't an animal in them. Probably stepped through one instead of pushing through. I found hairs, but no other sign. We'd reset them.

"Marshall, I'm going to head back. You want to come with me, or you ok out here?"

I didn't want to leave him alone, especially with Spider gunning for him.

"Sure," he said turning to follow me.

"Good. Did you have a good time last night?" I asked him innocently.

The young man's face burned bright red. "I didn't know that's what tickle fighting really was," he said after a moment.

"Sorry, I thought you might have," I said quietly, hoping he wasn't dying of embarrassment.

"Don't be sorry. I've never, I mean... Wow." His face was so red I thought his head was going to pop.

"Now you know why you're supposed to hang a hat," I told him, "so you don't get interrupted."

"I ... yeah. Lance always kept the girls away from me. Now I sort of understand why."

"He didn't want your feelings to be hurt?" I asked.

"Well, the naked part was a surprise, but what came after? Wow."

I chuckled. I'd left Raider back at the house with Mary who'd asked my Grandma to read to her since it was Marshall's off day for classes.

"Yeah. You know that's how babies are made, right?" I asked him.

"I know. I'm not worried about that. We were safe—"

"Listen," I told him, not turning, "I'm not going to ask you details other than, did you get her name?"

"Yeah, Erica. She wants to go with me on a walk later on. Do you think ... is that moving too fast?"

"That's up to you," I told him. "I'm guessing you've mostly had other people making decisions for you most of your life, right?"

"Mostly, yeah. Or they tell me what I should be doing, instead of doing something else. Like a morality thing. I was just wondering if this was a morality thing?"

"It is and it isn't," I told him. "Right now, the world is all topsy turvy. If you're asking my advice, I'll give it to you, but I won't tell you what to do."

"You know, that'd be easier. I feel..." he tapped his chest, making a fist out of his hand, "it's weird. Fun, exciting. And... I..."

"I know," I told him.

"I'd like your advice," he said as we broke cover from the woods and into the back of our ten acres.

"Well, if she makes you feel good, as long as it isn't hurting you or her or anybody else, I don't see a problem with it. People are social animals, and we're sort of drawn to those we're attracted to, whether or not we want that to happen."

"The attraction part doesn't bother me," Marshall said, "just ... never mind."

"Ok," I said, wondering if I had said something wrong or misunderstood him. "Looks like the kids aren't in Carla's classes today," I told him seeing three dogs chasing sticks to a gaggle of laughing and screaming children.

"Oh, I forgot, today would have been her and her husband's anniversary."

I winced; he'd been killed in the fighting. Every-body had lost somebody, and I feared it wasn't done and over with yet.

"Hey Spider, your dime," I told him, wondering what he wanted.

"It's been nearly a week," he said, his voice slow, "and it appears you've made your decision."

"It would appear so. More threats? Is that why you radioed?"

"No, just thought I'd update you on some goings. It seems a group has found out the locations of some of my pre-stashed supplies and stolen things. To make matters worse, the group set some clever traps and I lost several teams, including the ones I first set to retrieve things."

"Gosh, that really sucks. I hope whoever did it at least got the supplies out before your men blew them-selves up."

"Blew things up, eh?" he said smugly. "I thought it might have been you and yours."

I kicked myself. He'd said traps, and I'd all but confirmed my involvement. *Our* involvement. Did it matter? Maybe it wouldn't hurt for him to know he wasn't playing against a defenseless target for once.

"Well, bad things happen to bad people, and you're right up there with the evilest sadistic bastards to ever have lived. Can't say I'm sorry."

"You finish burying your dead, figuring out who we took?"

I ground my teeth. "Spider, as much as I like talking to you, what do you want? I'm sort of on a deadline here."

"Aren't you even curious how your people are doing?" he asked, his voice oily.

"Honestly?" I answered, lying through my teeth, "you took a bunch of malcontents, and there's a few I don't know or don't have an opinion about one way or another. Good thing too, you got some of the crybabies out of here."

People behind me paused. Linda and Jessica were trying to shoo them away, but it was starting to attract a crowd. I could see Sheriff Jackson walking in, his hand over his earpiece, his face stormy. He'd been listening in. I hoped he realized I was playing a game again, letting his nephew Deputy Rolston get some sort of background. Would he believe that?

"Malcontents, you're right about that. Several of your group have voiced their concerns, especially about your leadership. If you're so quick to throw their lives away, why do you personally take insane risks with little to no reward? I'm guessing it's because you either don't know, or I really did take those you despised."

"Projecting much?" I asked him. "So, you're here to try to twist me into knots, like the last time we talked? It won't work."

"Oh, I was rather hoping it would," Spider said softly.

"It would be foolish to try what you did again," I told him. "We now have protocols in place to keep things like that from happening again. You hit us, we hit you back. If you continue harassing the good people of this county, I'll hit you again. And again. I'll poison your water supply... I'll gas your men like I did at Henry's..."

I was going for threatening, but I let off the PTT to take a sip of water. Talking with pure evil and running a bluff was parching work. Raider pushed his head under my hand, trying to squeeze up on the bench between me and Jessica. I patted his head and pushed him back. Diesel and Yaeger were about ten feet away from her, holding the stay command she'd given them. The big dogs generally worked in tandem to keep people away.

"So that was you," he said softly.

"Yes, and you're all lucky I didn't use something nastier than Chlorine gas. I could have used Sulphur Mustard or Lewisite. Those two are pretty crude, but I can synthesize them in the barn with the equipment I have. Run a compressor into a holding tank... I could lob gas at you from afar and there wouldn't be a damned thing you could do about it if I decide to fight dirtier than we have been."

"You would surely kill the innocent with such a device," Spider said.

"And God would have to judge me for my actions,"

I shot back. "You've got the numbers, you've got equipment, but what you don't have is our ruthless nature to survive and live to be free."

"I will admit, I've been a little surprised at your resourcefulness."

"You've pushed us, and I've had enough. If you want all out warfare, it'll cost you dearly," I said, letting the button go. "By the way, your fuel dumps haven't been protected as well as they probably should have. A couple charges of thermite would be some tit for tat, and ironic, don't you think?"

Spider cursed over the airwaves. I grinned at that. The radio went silent as he broke the connection.

"Thermite?" the Sheriff asked me. "And how do you know about his fuel dumps?"

"We don't have anybody that close," Linda told him. "Wes is doing the same thing to Spider that he's been doing to us."

I turned to them. "Yeah, and I was trying to lay some cover, a background story to plant a seed of doubt about..."

"You know something?" Sheriff Jackson said, "You play bad cop really good. I could have sworn you were being serious." The last bit came out in a whisper.

"I think of what I really want to do, strip away the morality of the situation and be the monster the bad guys really are. Or at least they think I will be."

"That's sort of brilliant," Emily said from behind us.

"Thank you. Jessica and I have been talking about

how to sow doubt. I don't know why this fool keeps calling us. If he thinks we're just going to give everyone up just because he says so, he's crazy. He must have a reason, but I can't figure it out yet."

"Well, we've talked about it," Jess said, sitting on the bench next to me. "I still think that he's been trying to cause doubt and division here. At least with our core group."

"It's definitely amped up the paranoia," I told Jess softly.

"Yours or ours?" she asked.

Raider pushed his head under my hand again, so I gave him scratches while I considered how to answer.

"Everyone's," I told her.

29

MUCH TO THE amusement of the guys, and a couple of pouty faces from the gals, Marshall and Erica seemingly became inseparable. I'd kind of thought Emily would take it badly, but she was always smiling when they were around. Was that a real smile, or was she hiding her feelings?

"Penny for your thoughts," Jessica said, sitting down on the porch near me.

"You wouldn't have two cents to rub together," I told her.

"I doubt that. We broke Spider's code again. It sounds like he's been expecting that, so they really aren't trying very hard anymore. Your threat, though..." Jessica shivered.

"I know I promised you I wouldn't use gas," I told her.

"Right now, the threat of it is enough to keep them out of our areas. For some reason, he believes you're ruthless enough to go through with it. What I'm wondering is, if push came to shove, *are* you that ruthless?"

"I don't know," I told her. "Gas is... Innocent people would die, and I don't know if I can live with that."

"If we do nothing, innocent people are still dying. The men who are too old to work the fields are being either conscripted to work in their supplies, or they're being killed. Almost all the older women are being killed."

I was silent for a moment, digesting that information.

"So, by not moving on them, we're doing as much harm as if we'd gone through with my threats?" I asked her.

"I don't know. I know I made you promise but think I should take that back. Just in case. If you can really do it?"

"I can do it. It's kind of like what Jay Paulson learned in his training. He had to know how to make the bombs, set the traps first. It gave him an understanding he wouldn't have otherwise while he defused them. When I was in school it was kind of flip-flopped, but sorta the same. I had to learn what not to do, because it was dangerous. It was interesting reading, and I'm sure there's been a ton of backyard chemists who've done things like that—"

"Mister Wes?" Mary called running up, both Yaeger and Diesel chasing after the little girl happily.

BOYD CRAVEN III

"Hey sweet pea," I said as she came to a stop in front of both of us.

"Mister Marshall and Anthony got another pig!"

I stood up, a grin lighting my face. The last pig that we'd been smoking slowly for the last few days smelled heavenly.

"Did they shoot it?" I asked her.

"No, it's got that noose thingy on its neck. They're bringing it up here now!"

"Good!" I told her, "Is it a big one?"

"I don't know." She shrugged. "My mom went back with Miss Erica to talk to them and Miss Erica told me to come tell you. Mister Marshall wants your help in him learning how to..." She made a motion with her finger over her neck.

"Ok good. So, they're all back here?" I asked.

"Well, soon. My momma was walking back there to look at the traps. She wants to learn stuff too, she said."

"Where's my crazy mutt?" I asked her.

"He's in the barn with Miss Jessica's momma. She's giving him belly scratches."

I grinned. "Your mom's cheating on your pups."

"How do you figure?" Jess said bumping into me. "We're all gonna be related soon anyways."

"True, still, he should have been with Mary or me," I told her. "He should know—"

"He goes where he's needed," Jessica said softly. "Mom's been having a hard time lately. She's been missing Dad."

Her words turned somber at that and I put my arm

around her, pulling her close. "Hey sprout, you want to let Marshall know we'll make a class out of doing this?" I told her.

"A class?"

"I know I'm not the only one here who's processed game. I'd like to not be the one always doing it," I told her. "Besides, if something happened to me, they should know for themselves."

"Nothing's going to happen to you," Mary said, then launched herself into my lap, putting her arms around my chest in a hug, snaking them underneath Jessica's as well.

"I don't plan on it ever happening," I told her, "but you never know."

"Momma says you're too tough to get hurt for long."

I thought about my ankle; I could get around on it without the cane now, but for a while there I'd been worried I was going to be laid up for a long, long time.

"Yeah, but what if the bad guys took me?" I asked her, brushing her hair out of her face.

"Then you'd blow them up and get away. You're good at getting away."

"And getting yourself caught," Jessica said, a note of amusement in her voice.

I poked her in the side, making her jerk in surprise. "Now you guys are messing with me," I said, pulling the both of them into a bear hug.

"Too tight, you're squeezing my guts out!"

I let up a little bit, and she turned crawling onto

both mine and Jessica's laps, sort of laying across us. She put her head on her hands and stretched like a lazy cat would sitting in a sunny spot on the floor, before getting comfortable.

"I really like it here. Everybody treats me nice. You two are kind of like my aunt and uncle now, aren't you?"

Jessica's hand found mine while I stroked her hair. It was late afternoon, but the sun hadn't quite started setting yet. I waited, and bumped Jessica with my arm.

"I can't speak for Wes, but that's how I feel," Jessica told her, giving my hand a squeeze.

"You remember that morning Mister Lester gave you Ovaltine?"

"Yuck, yes, you fibbed and told me it was good!"

I chuckled. "You asked me if I was going to be your new daddy. You're probably too young to understand this, but I didn't know what I was feeling. Everything had gone so wrong, yet it'd gone so right. I'd just been hurt and was still recovering. Remember?"

"Your brains were mushed."

Jessica giggled.

"Yeah. And the reason I said no, I'm not a father … that's somebody special in your life, somebody who doesn't just get replaced easily." I realized with a start, I was talking to both ladies. "But if you need me, if you'd let me, I'd like to be an uncle figure, or a big brother, or whatever you need, kiddo. I love you to pieces."

"That's why you squish my guts out? Because I'm

pretty sure my guts wouldn't be all in pieces, they'd be a big glop of mush."

I grinned as she pushed my hand away and sat up before sliding down on the step below mine and called the dogs to her. Diesel came lumbering over and flopped on the bottom step in front of her. Yaeger came up past the little girl and gave Jessica a sniff on the side of the neck, then started licking her.

"Back off, ye foul hound," Jessica said in a mock English accent.

"Looks like somebody got jealous," I told her with a smile.

"Diesel likes me the best though," Mary piped up.

"As far as kids go, you're pretty much awesome-sauce," I told her.

She gave me a grin.

———

THE PIG WASN'T AS LARGE AS THE LAST ONE, BUT IT WAS impressive. This would definitely help, coupled with the stolen supplies. I didn't get my hands dirty this time and talked Marshall through it. Anthony was helping, and although he looked a little green around the gills, he didn't throw up. I didn't tell them that no matter how many animals I processed, during the first moments I always wanted to throw up. Just the way of life, something that I'd gotten a little bit numb from.

"Ok, now what do we do?" Marshall asked, his

arms covered in gore and bits of hair from the brindle-colored hog.

"Now you quarter it up and make your cuts." I walked him through it while a small crowd watched.

"Are we going to cook some up again tonight?" Grandma asked me from the chair I'd brought down off the porch for her.

"If you want," I told her. "Or we could get some of the ham out of the smoker and see if that's ready."

"Now I like that idea," Jess asked, rubbing her stomach. "Smoked ham, bacon..."

A SCENE THAT HAD PLAYED OUT HERE MORE OFTEN lately than not, the entire small community at my Grandma's farm ... my farm? were sitting around the cookfire once again. Our core group shared the latest news, most of the questions regarding Spider and what could we do. We answered as much as we dared, but it was watered down. I was still paranoid. Spider knew things he shouldn't, and there was still a mole here to be found out. Our attempt to flush out the traitor hadn't worked, but we'd stung Spider and put a seed of doubt into his thoughts.

"Can I save some for my mom?" Mary asked Jessica and me. We'd been handing out plates of sliced and smoked ham to go with the nonstop soup pot.

"Yeah, where is she?" I asked her, puzzled.

"I don't know. She hasn't come back yet?" Her words were puzzled.

"Marshall, Anthony?" I called loudly; the darkness was only held at bay by the crackling of a low burning cookfire.

"Sir!" "Yes, Mister Wes?" they called.

"Did you see Emily?"

"Yes," Anthony said stepping towards the fire. "Why, what's wrong?"

The young man's eyes were suddenly wary as he looked around the now silent crowd.

"Marshall?"

"She was going to look at the traps. She had her big pistol, lever gun and a backpack. I think she was going to put some more out. I'm not sure."

"Has anybody seen her since?" I asked, feeling a note of panic.

Nobody answered.

"Has *anybody* seen Emily since Marshall and the boys dragged this hog back?"

Thundering silence.

Had she been snagged?

Sheriff Jackson stepped forward into the light. "I need two teams. Marshall and Anthony will work with one, I'll work with Wes with the other. Flashlights if you have them."

"She's gone?"

"Maybe she's lost?"

"Did the bad men get her?"

"Did she leave?"

"What if she's been working for the bad guys all along?"

The murmurs were low, but every single one of them was heard by me. I shuddered.

"Mary, how about you and Grandma go talk with Miss Carpenter? See if she can get her on the radio?"

"Did she take a radio?" Jess asked me.

"We're lousy with them now, she usually has one," I told her.

"Ok Mister Wes, come on Grandma, want me to have one of the boys bring your chair back up for you?"

"How about we see if I have any of the cornbread cookie cakes left?" Grandma asked.

Her recipe was an evolution in progress. We had lots of things to bake with, but cornbread had always been a staple. Add in dried fruits to the batter, fry them in a pan like a pancake... Not everything Grandma cooked was delicious. This wasn't horrible.

"Ok. Joey!" Mary yelled, "Carry Grandma's chair up with me?"

"Yes Miss Mary," the boy said sweetly.

He had to have been going on ten, but Mary and he had been thick as thieves and she liked to boss him around. Apparently, he didn't mind being bossed. If I wasn't being eaten away by panic, I might have found that endearing.

"And Mister Wes, I think maybe my mom got lost. You've been really good about finding things. Find my mommy for me?"

"Sure, thing sweetie. How about you bunk out on the couch tonight? I'll have your mom come in and get you, or you both can crash out there when we find her."

"Ok."

The crowd hadn't moved off, but they weren't as densely packed as the folks started organizing themselves.

30

"SILENT HUNTER, COME IN," Linda's voice came out of the radio.

"Silent here, any word?" I asked.

She'd been trying to raise Emily on the radio, at least on the channels that we didn't think Spider had broken the codes to. We didn't want to broadcast on an open frequency, but we also didn't know if she'd been snatched by his men.

"It's something else. I need you back here. I'm recalling all teams."

We'd ended up with three search parties.

"Can you say over the channel what's going on?" I asked.

"No."

Next to me, Jessica grunted in response. I felt a cold chill run through me.

"WHAT IS IT?" I ASKED. RAIDER PANTED FROM HIS OWN run to try to keep up with me. I'd run far ahead of anybody else, even Jessica.

She'd wanted me to slow, but if somebody had found Emily's body, I knew I needed to be there for Mary. Emily had been funny lately. She'd been so happy, too many smiles. I'd watched her attention change from me to Marshall, and for Marshall to fall head over heels, or in lust ... with another woman. I knew the rejection had to hurt, that and she wasn't the most stable woman out there. I'd seen her execute two men at the drop of a dime, yet she was a good mother. I'd started running hard when I'd remembered her words from the night we'd had to sedate her.

"I don't know if I'm cut out for this world anymore," she said softly.

"We found a note, here in her bunk," Linda said, handing me a page of yellow lined paper.

WES,

I hate to do this, but it's tearing me up inside. I have to go away for a while. Please remember your promise about Mary. She loves you, more so than her own father. I'm sorry things wouldn't have worked out between us, but if I don't come back, I want you to keep her safe for me the way a parent would. I'm not sure I can keep myself together, and she shouldn't have to grow up seeing me coming apart.

I hope you're not mad at me. The worst day of my life was the day you yelled at me and made me realize how horrible I am for my daughter. I needed to hear that, which is why I'm leaving. I need to make peace with whatever it is that's wrong with me.

Don't come looking for me, you won't find me easily. I want to be left on my own, and don't worry about me doing something stupid. I've got my BFR and lever gun with me. I'll be safe, and if it's God's will, I'll be back to the homestead sooner or later.

Always,

Emily

"What is it? Jessica asked a moment later.

I handed her the note. I was shaking. She read it quickly, her face turning a furious shade of red. Her hands shook. She dropped the note on the table next to her mom.

"That selfish bitch," Jessica swore.

"I heard Raider barking; did you find my mommy?" Mary asked, the light from inside the barn illuminating the little girl who'd wandered in.

I stammered for an answer.

"Honey, come here," Jessica said, patting the bench beside her mother. "We've got to talk."

--THE END --

To be notified of new releases, please sign up for my mailing list at: http://eepurl.com/bghQb1--

ABOUT THE AUTHOR

Boyd Craven III was born and raised in Michigan, an avid outdoorsman who's always loved to read and write from a young age. When he isn't working outside on the farm, or chasing a household of kids, he's sitting in his Lazy Boy, typing away.

You can find the rest of Boyd's books on Amazon & Select Book Stores.

boydcraven.com
boyd3@live.com

Made in United States
North Haven, CT
04 February 2022

15717665R00168